NAOMI ISHIGURO

ESCAPE ROUTES

TINDER
PRESS

First published in Great Britain in 2020 by Tinder Press
An imprint of HEADLINE PUBLISHING GROUP

First published in paperback in 2021 by Tinder Press
An imprint of HEADLINE PUBLISHING GROUP

Molly Aitken's interview with Naomi Ishiguro appears
by kind permission of *Cunning Folk*

1

Cataloguing in Publication Data is available from the British Library

ISBN 978 1 4722 6486 2

Designed and typeset by EM&EN
Printed and bound in Great Britain by Clays Ltd, Elcograf S.p.A.

MIX
Paper from
responsible sources
FSC® C104740

HEADLINE PUBLISHING GROUP
An Hachette UK Company
Carmelite House
50 Victoria Embankment
London EC4Y 0DZ

www.tinderpress.co.uk
www.headline.co.uk
www.hachette.co.uk

For my parents,
and for Ben

Contents

Wizards

Alfie was heading over the pebbled dunes of Brighton beach towards the ice-cream stall when a red-headed boy with a Frisbee hurtled into him, knocking them both to the ground. Alfie stopped himself crying out just in time and tried his best to smile instead, because this kid was from that big group he'd noticed splashing together all puppy-like by the waves, yelling odd and mysterious things like *In your face!* and *Bangarang!* at each other, while laughing for what seemed like no reason at all.

'Hello,' he said to this boy with the Frisbee.

'Hi,' said the boy, somehow back on his feet and set to dash off already, his eyes on the big crowd of friends that were waiting and waving by the shoreline. He hurled the Frisbee off in their direction – a bright splash of orange against the blue, blue sky – before finally turning to Alfie.

'Why're you dressed like that?' was all he said. 'You look really strange.'

And then he was off, back to the others, leaving Alfie to pick himself up off the uncomfortable pebbles and brush down the trousers and striped shirt Mum had bought specially for coming on holiday.

But it didn't matter, Alfie told himself. Those kids didn't really look like much fun anyway. They were probably all younger than him, for one thing, and most likely quite boring when you got past their loudness and their smiles. Loud children often were. And then what would Mum have said if he'd just given up on the ice-cream mission and gone off to play with them? If he'd simply bounded off to the waves, jumping into all that noise and the shrieking laughing sounds and the mess of the fine shingle kicked up – *It'll get in your eyes,* she would have said, *or worse, you'll get it in someone else's eyes.* If he'd run towards the glitter of water scattered through the air from dancing fingertips, catching the light of this unseasonably blazing April day – *It'll wash away the sun block,* she would have said, *and do we know what that means? That means skin cancer, Alfie, love, and then who'll be laughing?*

Except Alfie had no idea who would be laughing. Probably these kids, still splashing like a pack of puppies at the water's edge of Brighton beach while he lay in a spotted hospital gown on a hospital bed plugged into one of those vast machine thingies with all the tubes connected, like you see in movies and TV shows when people are sick. And his head would be bald like all the cancer children they show during *Comic Relief* and *Children in Need,* because Alfie would be a cancer child, like Mum said, while these children were still playing.

But he was wasting time. Mum and Wallace would be wondering where he was. He shook himself and started to walk again across the beach to the ice-cream stand, and yet it was harder than it looked with his feet sinking deep into the heaped beach pebbles, and with people and blankets and beach things everywhere.

If it really came to it, though, he considered as he walked, and he did become a cancer child, he would just have to make sure he survived until he was eleven and his magic powers kicked in. Then he could have lessons and figure out how to heal himself, because wizards like he would be (he doubted whether those other kids – the laughing doggy ones – were also wizards) didn't get cancer, or if they did they didn't have cancer for long because they possessed miraculous powers of self-healing. And so really, Alfie realised, due to his latent wizardness, it didn't matter at all about the sun block or staying away from the water, and Mum was wrong – completely wrong.

But then red-faced Wallace would inevitably back her up about it, and it would be such an effort to explain and to argue with the two of them calling him *wilful*, and *disobedient*, and *hard work* that maybe he wouldn't bother. Being honest with himself, he thought perhaps it would be better to wait until he actually was eleven before he truly abandoned sun block because he didn't want to be a cancer child without the magic healing powers yet. He would bide his time. He could be wise like that. He was wise beyond his years, Miss Lennox often said at school. He liked Miss Lennox, in spite of her strange teeth and the way she couldn't pronounce the letter 's', saying it instead like a 'th'. Poor Miss Lennox. It would be sad to leave her in ten months when he became a wizard. But then it would be worse to leave her as a cancer child, so maybe obey the sun block rules. No sea. No splashing. No dancing and yelling at the water's edge. He could wait.

Alfie turned from watching the other kids to trudge up the last bit of beach, and soon found himself blinking up at the ice-cream seller, a ragged-faced man with a spike through one earlobe.

'Two 99 Flakes, please,' he said. 'And one lemon sorbet.'

*

Luciano the Diviner, also known as Peter – also sometimes known as *dude* or *buddy* to the stoners of Brighton beach, owing to the fact of his being a twenty-eight-year-old white man with dreadlocks who consistently wore flip-flops regardless of the season – stood in the dark of his fortune-telling booth, gathering keys, wallet, sunglasses and bandanna. He was closing up early today in order to give himself the chance to drink it all in – to catch some rays, chill for a bit, and be in sync with the beauty of the Universe before the sun went down and the night set in. It would be a crime, almost, not to make the most of it all, it being only April and yet magically warm, even for the South Coast – even for Brighton with its famous microclimate. Ah, the Brighton microclimate. Of course, Luciano the Diviner/Peter always nodded sagely whenever it was mentioned and insisted on its being a thing, along with everyone else in the city, but really, if he was honest? Brighton seemed as grey to him as any other part of England.

He forgot himself a moment and hummed out loud a random section of 'The Great Gig in the Sky' as he pushed his bandanna back over his enormous hair (*Christ*, said the small voice in his head that often sounded annoyingly like his dad, *not exactly Frank Sinatra, are you?*) . . . oh, but what had he been thinking about before? Before Pink Floyd and his dad and his own awful singing voice? The Brighton microclimate, the unseasonable weather . . . and the Universe! That had been it. The Universe. This was not a day for worrying at all, but for appreciating how lucky, how blessed he was to belong to that universal, so to speak, all-loving mother. He was a child of the Universe just like anybody else, and that was one good thing he had going for him, if nothing further, and his dad could go to hell if he didn't accept that. He wedged his sunglasses somewhere up into his mess of dreads and bandanna, slid his feet into his flip-flops, and stepped out of the booth on to the tarmac. And amen to all that, he considered, not precisely knowing what he was saying amen to, he'd become so disoriented by the sun and its sudden warmth on his skin.

It had been a long winter – the worst since 1996, people said, the last time Jupiter had spent three weeks of February in misalignment with Saturn, and Mercury in retrograde. Or was it Venus, in fact, that had been out of alignment with Saturn? He couldn't quite remember at this point, but that was maybe it. That, or it was all a question of perspective and it was actually Saturn that had been out of alignment with Venus, and Mercury hadn't had much to do with things at all. He'd have to look it up later, tonight, and yet . . . and yet it felt so *wrong* to be wrecking his head with all this difficult, almost academic thought when look! Here was Brighton, lit up in all its glory. Legendary city, meeting place of sparring mods and rockers looking epic on motorcycles (though, *Those fumes are bad for Mother Earth, dudes*, he always shouted from his skateboard every time he passed them in the line-up with their bikes every convention), home to the celebrated Royal Pavilion (weird, colonial, a little bit gaudy), and wellspring of decades' worth of dirty picture postcards sold on seafront stands to be sent to friends and relatives for miles around (with captions that always, if he was honest, made him cringe a little). But it was still a pretty awesome place overall, he reflected, as he pulled down the iron shutters on his booth. This Brighton, this city, this adopted home of his. He'd better hurry up and get involved; he only had five hours or so before it would start to get dark.

'Hello,' said a female voice located somewhere behind him just as he was turning the key. 'Are you closing for lunch or coffee or, you know, for a few minutes while you go buy something or whatever, or is that like *it*, and I've clean missed my chance to have my fortune read today?'

She was American and pretty. Charming smile – lots of work done on those teeth, and maybe some on her face, too. That is to say, she wasn't young, exactly. Not old, either, not by any means, but a good few years older than Luciano/Peter, that was certain. There was one thing about her, though, that really struck him as she stood before him, blinking in the shadow of his fortune-telling booth. She was exactly the right height.

To be clear, Luciano/Peter wasn't particularly short. In fact, it was only because the people in England were so freakishly tall that he ever, in some rare contexts, appeared small at all. In Japan, for instance, the place in the world he had always considered his true spiritual home, Luciano/Peter would probably be of comfortably average height. Unless of course the people of Japan had all started eating terrible capitalist junk food pumped full with growth hormones like they did in the West. Never having actually been to Japan he couldn't say what they ate, really, or how tall they were as a result, but what he did know for certain – it was so obvious, so clear and without question – was that this pretty American woman blinking up at him now was just tall enough that if, hypothetically, he were to enfold her in a tender embrace (*Don't flatter yourself, son*, said that fatherly voice in his head again. *She wouldn't look at you twice if she knew the first thing about you*) he would be able to rest his chin quite comfortably on the very top of her beautiful tousled head. She seemed like she could be from California, he thought, like The Beach Boys and O'Neill and the end of Route 66. They were kindred spirits, obviously.

'Uh,' said Luciano/Peter. 'There's another guy, just down the promenade. Sapphire Blue. He does fortunes too.'

So maybe they were kindred spirits, but he was nervous, OK? It's not every day the Universe deposits a beautiful woman of exactly the right height, who somehow also wants to talk to you, just bang outside your workplace.

'That's too bad,' said the woman, chewing on her thumbnail. 'My friend told me you were the man to see. The best in all of Brighton, she said.'

He looked out at the sloping expanse of sun-warmed shingle and sand, and at all the holiday people who were already basking in the freedom of it all, already rejoicing in the scene stretched out before them. He looked back at the woman. She was fiddling with a pendant now – amethyst, he noted – that was resting against the freckled skin of her décolletage.

'That your birthstone?' he asked.

She nodded. 'Aquarius,' she said. 'Venus rising.'

He was Libra. It was perfect.

He flashed her his best beatific smile and chanced a hand upon her upper arm. Her skin was warm and firm and slightly moist, and he guessed that if he took his hand away and licked his fingers he'd taste salt. (*Disgusting,* piped up his father's voice, again.) But this was what you had to do, wasn't it? In those rare moments the Universe presented you with something so obvious, so *right*, so synchronous as this.

'If that's the case,' he said, slipping the key back into the lock for the shutters and opening the booth up again – dreamcatchers, star maps, Indian silks of different colours; he hoped she'd be impressed! – 'I think I can make an exception.'

*

Back on the blanket with Mum and Wallace, Alfie took a moment to celebrate (quietly, with no loud or outward displays of boisterousness) the sheer successfulness of everything. Because the ice creams had been returned with no spillages, no droppages, and no reasons for him to be termed *wilful* or *disobedient* or *hard work*! Praise be to the spike-eared ice-cream man and his ingenious cardboard contraption, allowing for the easeful transportation of more than one cone at a time. Thanks to him, Alfie's mission status was complete. And he'd passed with flying colours, as Miss Lennox would say. She often told him things like that, things he didn't fully understand but thought most beautiful in any case, perhaps even a little because he didn't understand.

Flying colours. Down the beach a green and purple kite fluttered up to the blue sky trailing a silver-spangled tail. Staring hard, Alfie found the kite's twine – a thin ghost of a line through the air – and followed it down through the mess of the crowds to a girl in a yellow dress. How amazing that he'd found this kite and this girl just as he'd focused on those words – *flying colours*! As if he'd summoned them by magic, almost, without precisely meaning to. The girl was a few years older than him, it seemed. She was a lot taller, at least. He blurred his eyes as he watched her until she became a simple splash of yellow, the perspective messing with the scale of things until she was like a daffodil. He started on his ice cream.

Flying colours. When Miss Lennox had handed back the maths tests, moving from desk to desk in the disinfectant-smelling maths room – shoes still clicky as usual but muted on the dull green floor tiles – she'd paused a moment by Alfie's desk before placing that perfect thing before him, his completed test with workings and answers written calmly and neatly – as if he'd progressed through the questions with a calm assurance like Blofeld in *Thunderball* (though actually he'd been nervous; he always was somehow when Miss Lennox was involved, even though of course he loved her) – and with a whole column of red ticks lined up alongside his neat answers and workings, each tick perfectly regular, mirroring the dependable correctness of his answers, all stacked up one on top of the other, tidy as a block of flats. *Flying colours*, she'd said to him then. And how Alfie had danced when he'd got home to his room that night! How he'd whirled and dived and hurled himself with triumph to lie stretched out on the covers of his bed, closing his eyes against the boring, plaster-peeling ceiling as if against the brightness of the sun, and finding blue and pink and lilac and gold behind his eyelids, flying all around him like energised lashings of paint, like parrots' wings, like the parachute silk from the cat and mouse game at Imogen's birthday. If he were to go there again, go back to Imogen's birthday after this wonderful thing of the column of red ticks from Miss Lennox and the flying colours, he would wheel and shriek under the parachute with the best of them and never worry about what would happen if he were to skid in his socks – if he were to fall and wear out the knees of his trousers and then get a bruise or a graze or a tear in his shirt that would make Mum look so weary and so disappointed – he wouldn't worry about anything at all and so would laugh even louder than anyone else when he was caught and lost the game. Louder and louder than anyone else until he drowned them all out, in the same way that this thought of Miss Lennox and the flying colours was drowning out the shouts and laughs of the other children still all together at the waves' edge. That was a kind of magic, too, Alfie thought: his ability to do this, this drowning out, this flying.

'Alfie, love. You're ruining your shirt,' said meat-handed Wallace. And for once he was right. So distracted had Alfie become by fond memories and recollections of past glory, he'd allowed the 99 Flake in his right hand to drip all down the sleeve of his new shirt. None of the other kids on the beach were wearing shirts, of course, so it wouldn't matter if they spilt their ice creams. They were wearing swimming costumes and had their limbs exposed, like trees. Because did you know that *limbs* as a word comes from trees, having been used in the past by olden-times people when referring to branches, meaning that people and trees were somehow magically linked? Alfie hadn't known it, not until Miss Lennox had told him, and he thought it wonderful. Probably that was what true magic would be about, when the time came for him to learn it properly – nothing stupid and kid-ish like *hocus pocus* or *abracadabra*, or any rubbish that a simple party entertainer could do. Instead it would be based on his insightful perceptions of the unlikely correspondences between things, and Miss Lennox would teach him more about this next year, when he needed to learn to use his powers properly. He so hoped that were true. Then maybe he wouldn't have to leave her. Because what would life be like, really, with no more Miss Lennox in it? It was horrible to think, when *flying colours* and everything it hinted at, everything it meant, seemed to fade when she wasn't around, even just in the holidays.

'Alfie,' Mum said. 'Pay attention.'

Alfie licked off the top layer of his sun-melted ice cream and tried to smile at her. She only stared back, biting hard into her scoop of lemon sorbet, which was somehow both lurid and pale at the same time, and so cold-looking he couldn't see how she could be eating it so quickly like that without getting toothache, or stomach ache, or certainly without making her endless headache worse. And how could eating like that be any kind of fun? He wanted to tell her to stop and to tell her about Miss Lennox and about tree limbs and people limbs, but it seemed like an awful lot, suddenly, to say all at once – to get ordered in words and to explain in a way that wouldn't be annoying – so he just smiled and smiled, and Mum kept biting into her block-of-ice sorbet, and told him through the cold of it: 'You've got bits of chocolate in your teeth.'

*

'You have such a compassionate energy,' said the American woman to Luciano the Diviner as they sat in the cramped and glittered darkness of his fortune-telling booth. 'Has anyone ever told you that?'

Luciano/Peter considered all the people he had known in his life. So many beautiful souls, come to think of it. So many, in such a comparatively short time. Could that be normal? Was he not blessed? Although perhaps it wasn't completely out of the question to suggest that he himself might have had a hand in filling his world up with such good people, because they did say, after all, that you got from the Universe what you gave out, and that you saw in the world the details you wanted to see, and, in short, that life was what you made of it. And he didn't know what else he gave out if not love, pure unconditional love, like Jesus did, in fact, because though of course not a Christian – no way, organised religion being harmful bullshit, obviously – Jesus was the man, you know? Just that one particular dude, he was such a spiritual soul, like Gandhi, or the Dalai Lama, or, like Bob Geldof, maybe, and it was heart-breaking what they did with all his teaching. It would undoubtedly have made him sad. But getting back to all the many good souls he'd known in his life. All he meant was that perhaps it wasn't just blind luck. Maybe it was even something for him to be a little proud of, because the thing was, he *noticed*: he saw the goodness and the beauty in people and, not to be self-aggrandising or anything, but maybe not everybody did. Maybe that was something that distinguished him a little from being just another dropout selling something dubious out of a spangled hut – this ability to perceive the awesome in people. What was that Hindu greeting? *Namaste*. The awesome in me salutes the awesome in you. So yes, he did deserve it all – all these beautiful souls who had appeared in his life – and who in hell cared what his father had to say about it anyway?

'Luci?' said the beautiful woman still right in front of him, for she called him Luci now, apparently. 'Luci? Are you OK, honey? Did I say something wrong?'

'Oh,' he replied, 'no, I'm sorry. I just thought I felt something there. I was riding the wave of the feeling, you know?'

'God, I *do* know,' she said. 'Happens to me literally all the time. Always tough explaining without just sounding crazy, though, right?'

My god, she was perfect. She understood everything, as well as being exactly the right height. But she had her palms up on the table now, he noticed, and extended to him – her beautiful palms like an offering. And Luciano/ Peter was suddenly aware of his having mentioned that he could do her a palm reading after the Tarot reading and star chart they had already done . . . But hang on, thinking about it, they must have been holed up like this together in the tiny booth for ages, for an hour or more, and still she hadn't tired of him or come to despise him or decided she'd prefer to wander by the waves in the beautiful sunlit day instead of being crammed into this tiny incense-stuffy booth. In fact, come to think of it now, why on earth *were* they crammed up in the booth when they could be outside, turning their laughing eyes upon one another in the thrown light of the afternoon sun?

Luciano/Peter hovered his palms over Agnes' out-stretched ones – her name was Agnes, he'd discovered, and actually she was from Ohio, not California – and after a moment of feeling the energy coursing between them he lowered his hands to hers. How essential, how truly magic it was to be able to connect like this to a whole other person, a whole other living human being with a world inside themselves just like he had, all through a simple touch of hands.

'Let's go outside,' he said. 'We can walk down to the sea and then I'll read your palm there in the light, where I'll be able to see every tiny indentation, every whisper of suggestion on your skin.'

'I was so hoping you'd say that,' said Agnes. How perfect! She even bore with him when he accidentally waxed poetic.

Together they abandoned the booth, and Luciano/ Peter felt so happy that he didn't even close the shutters because it wasn't going to rain and who in hell was going to rob him anyway when any passing fool could see he had nothing, absolutely nothing at all, to show for himself? (*Nothing material, Dad*, Luciano/Peter retorted back in his head, because there was no room for doubters today.)

'You were so right, Luci,' Agnes said once she was outside, stretching her arms and her hands and her long, expressive fingers up into the air. 'It's too gorgeous out here to ignore.'

You're too gorgeous to ignore, he nearly replied. But instead he told her: 'Call me Peter. That's my real name.'

They walked together out over the heaped, tumbling dunes at the back of the long sweep of beach, and he realised how much more clearly he could see her out here in the light, in the low golden afternoon sunlight – how long had they been talking? – but regardless of that, now they were out of the shadows of the booth he couldn't help but notice that Agnes – she of Ohio and not of California – was possibly a good bit older than he'd initially supposed. When first she'd stood before him as he'd been locking up he'd just been stunned to find a woman with an aura such as hers who was happy to speak to him (*because why would any woman bother, frankly, with that hair, and those clothes, and that job, and radiating lowlife deadbeat as you seem so set on doing?*). And probably he'd been a bit sun-dazzled and preoccupied – though he couldn't remember now with exactly what – so he'd just stared and perceived the simple fact of beauty instead of noticing the details. But now, having become more acclimatised to the presence of Agnes at his side, he noticed the lines around her eyes, the slight looseness of the skin around her collar-bones, the sunspots on her upper arms. She could be over forty, very easily – forty-five, or forty-seven, even. Did that matter? Was that weird? A reason to declare a spanner in the works of his perfect afternoon? (*She's just messing with you, son. I mean, she's seen the world a bit, she's been around, she knows what you are, don't kid yourself she's interested.*) No, Peter decided. It wouldn't matter if Agnes was fifty or fifty-nine or seventy – or OK, maybe not seventy, at least this would have to be a very different thing if she were seventy – but the point was it made her more beautiful, the fact that she had lived and seen something of the world and felt all kinds of things. Because that could only ever make a person more beautiful, not less, and his dad was just a bitter asshole anyway. He loved her laughter lines like he would love his own one day. (*Keep telling yourself that, son.*)

In defiance, then, he took her hand in his. And she looked at him, surprised but not repelled, and he towed her down the pebbly dunes and on to the wave-flattened sand. Low tide, the newly exposed beach a gleaming mirror for the sky, and so much space! Here were dogs, and children, and couples and families with stripy windbreaks, and over there was that ice-cream vendor, that dude with the earring, and Peter kind of wanted Agnes to buy him an ice cream for some reason, wasn't that funny? But they were part of it, he was part of it, and not as the weird fortune-teller with the dreads, looking on from the booth, but as Peter, flip-flops abandoned, leaping barefoot through the afternoon with a genuine smile and a girl – no, a woman – on his arm like the kind of man he'd always wanted to be. And it was easy, really. He didn't know what had stopped him before . . .

But hang on, here was some kid walking up to him, and with such purpose in his eyes. Did Peter know this kid? No, he didn't think he did know this kid, and yet still the kid approached. The kid, it seemed, had even abandoned his mother to march up to him like this because that was her, surely, calling after him now, that sad-faced woman over there by the waves with the shrivelled-up look and the tangled grey hair, who made Peter think of Dettox and oven gloves, of electric blankets and those awkward armband things they'd made him wear in the pool as a child

. . . and he had such *sympathy* with her, suddenly, though she frightened him, too, this woman, this kind of person he would absolutely never want to be – please never let him end up like this woman – oh, but it was silly to worry, of course, because Agnes would save him.

'Alfie!' called the woman, and her voice was as tired as the skin on her face.

And here was the kid – here was Alfie – right in front of him now.

'Mum, come and see,' Alfie was calling back to the woman over his shoulder. 'I've found him! I think I've found the wizard.' And then the kid broke off, and turned to Peter, looking him square in the eye in a way Peter would never have dared do to an adult when he'd been that age. 'At least, you are a wizard, aren't you?' the kid said then. 'It's just you look so much like one, with your cloak like that and everything.'

Gulls wheeled in the sky in circles up above them, and somewhere a baby was screaming. Peter dropped Agnes' hand to stare down at his blue and silver-threaded kaftan, at the amulets around his neck, at the leather thongs around his wrists, at the coloured rings on all his fingers and – *too much*, he thought, *ridiculous*. Maybe even absurd. Because this always happened. Not this specifically, of course, but just . . . everyone else *knowing* – effortlessly understanding what was needed from them in the world, understanding what was appropriate, what would command a degree of respect – while he Peter was uncertain and left behind. *Preposterous*, was what this kid was telling him. *You look preposterous*, and yet it wasn't fair! It wasn't fair at all because he couldn't be preposterous, not completely. Because Agnes hadn't blanched and pleaded a migraine or a previous appointment when he'd taken up her hand, had she? She'd gripped it back. This kid was wrong. And why was he staring at him like that now? As if seeing something in him he had no right to see?

'No, I'm not a fucking wizard,' Peter's voice said, seemingly of its own accord. He listened to its echo in his ears. 'What are you, five?'

Maybe it was spiteful. Peter wasn't often spiteful, at least not deliberately, so he wasn't too familiar with what it felt like, but yeah, probably it was spiteful because look, look at Alfie's face, there, crumbling. Look at Alfie running away from him now, sprinting up the beach, into the tangled crowds. Look at Alfie's sad, tired mother, standing there with her hand extended, calling, 'Alfie, Alfie,' as if she'd already given up.

*

Sprinting through legs, arms, heads and faces turning to admire how fast he was, like Sonic, like Road Runner, like that guy in that film that time – what was it? *Forrest*

Gump. Run, Forrest, run! No more careful picking of his way around the clutter, over the pebbles, Alfie flew through blankets, books, buckets and bottles.

All these other people on the beach! Other families, and other gatherings and groupings . . . just in time he jumped over a gritty sand sculpture of something like a cat with an acne-ridden teenager beside it wielding palette knives and brushes . . . all these people who did things so differently from Mum and Wallace – Mum and Wallace who spent so much time just *sitting* in the flat back home and staring at people buying things on TV when other people had more children and wheeled them in buggies to the park and to museums, and then when they were grown up enough to tease and play and create kerfuffle in airports they'd take them all to France, where they'd hire a big villa with a pool for the children to swim in all day long and where he, Alfie, would swim too with all the other kids while Mum and Wallace did . . . but he didn't know what Mum and Wallace would do.

He ran past a half-eaten hotdog lying abandoned between two families' territories, being picked at by gulls. He ran past the girl in the yellow dress he had seen with the kite – she was sitting with other girls now, chatting and sharing out sweets. Except the thing was, to be honest, the problem with the villa in France was that Alfie never swam. Not that he couldn't, he knew *how*, of course – Mum had made sure he'd had a few lessons just for safety's sake, in case of sudden and bad situations, maybe like *Titanic* or *James and the Giant Peach* or *Jaws* – but, well, the thing was that there was this hole in his eardrum they'd found one day at the doctor's, and the lessons had stopped after that . . . although, come to think of it, he couldn't feel the hole at all now; he felt fine. And surely he would feel it if it were really still there? Feel it now, for instance, while running? And hear the air and the wind whistling through it. Surely it would whistle quite loudly, maybe like an actual person whistling? *Stop making that noise!* Mum always said when Alfie tried whistling, because of her headache – and, *You pay attention now, Alfie,* Wallace always said after. *You listen to your mother, you do what she says.*

Alfie loved Mum, and he didn't want to leave her behind down the beach when he knew how bad the headache would get as a result of his running and leaving, but she'd told him she'd said he was going to a new school next term. No Miss Lennox, she'd said, and bigger classes, the mortgage and the Mastercard, and until Wallace gets a job again, and it wouldn't be too much further away from home and you never knew, maybe in the new school he'd make friends that much more easily . . . and so many things, so many things about that had made him want to shout (or to cry, because *even real men cry sometimes*, Wallace had said last year when Alfie had come into the kitchen after midnight because the water in the upstairs tap was broken) and this was better than shouting at her, probably, better than shouting, this running away.

He was running faster now, and right down by the waves where it was smooth and sandy and no one was in his way and all the people on the beach were just a jumbled blur of sound and colour way up the sloping shore beside him. How could he have made her see that maybe things would be all right when he was just a little older? That maybe even something completely unexpected would hit them then, a bolt from the blue: maybe something like a wizard stepping into their lives with new worlds or solutions, maybe even Alfie finding the magic powers that had been hidden (why so hidden?) in him somehow this whole time? A few years ago she might have listened, but something about the way life was for them now made that kind of thing sound foolish and kid-ish when said out loud, and anyway, him having faith like that in random forces could sometimes get Wallace's goat, as he called it, because Wallace didn't believe in any kind of magic. But forgetting Wallace, Alfie had just been stuck for a way to make Mum see that things always could get brighter, which was when the wizard had appeared, jumping down the dunes like a sign, like a way he maybe could explain to her, like the beginning of all the things he hoped for . . . But then, well, then it had all gone wrong, hadn't it, and he couldn't stay, he couldn't, because he couldn't shout or cry or make her sad because she always had a headache and now with the mortgage and the Mastercard and Wallace's job they'd probably never go on holiday like this again.

And here he was still running, though the crowds had thinned out on this part of the beach, which made him wonder why more people didn't come down this way, when it wasn't that much further along. Maybe they liked to be all crammed together, so that kids like those happy puppy kids he'd seen by the waves could jostle and giggle and splash with each other. And it was also, he supposed, much less of a walk to the ice-cream place from back down there in the crowds than it would be all the way from this bit of the beach. If they'd put their blanket down here and he'd gone to get ice cream for Mum and for Wallace then their cones would have melted down his sleeve, certainly, and all over his shirt by the time he would have been able to get back to the blanket. Yes, he was fast and yes, he was willing (though sometimes *hard work*), but running with ice creams would be difficult, even with one of those cardboard contraptions the spike-eared man had.

As Alfie slowed to a jog, the world seemed suddenly lovely, everything around him open space: a long stretch of sand ahead of him, flatish waves with unbroken horizon out beyond, and the shouts and laughs of the other families getting faint behind him, a bit like when stomach ache is nearly gone and you can read and forget about it for chapters at a time. And here was a woman out walking a dog. *Hello!* He waved to her. *Hello!* She waved back. He carried on jogging down the beach, taking longer strides, as long as his legs would allow, enjoying the feeling of strength that it gave him and the sensation of running on watercolour with the flat, wet sand beneath him all streaked with colours of reflected sunset.

There was hardly anyone left around here at all now. Only that tent over there and a man sitting outside who looked homeless, a little bit.

'Hello!' Alfie called to the man, as he jogged past.

'Alright,' said the man, raising a hand in greeting.

People were mostly kind, Alfie considered. And if they weren't, if they were angry like that wizard man had been, maybe it was because they had a headache or a mortgage – and in any case it was a whole ten months until Alfie's birthday when he turned eleven. The wizard had been unprepared, that was all, and may have even put Alfie off on purpose because they weren't meant to meet each other yet, not like that. It was too soon, still not time for magic or destiny.

No people at all now, and white cliffs instead. He could see them just a little further on, pale and powdery as giant broken pieces of blackboard chalk. Other than that it was just sea and sky and gulls, and also something concrete

up ahead, which he was running towards . . . but what
was it? Something stretching out to sea like a curved, grey
pier, like a road that went nowhere, like a wall, like something, something to protect . . . But it was sea defences; of
course that's what it was! Sea defences for a harbour, like
in Geography, like what Lucas sees at Scarrow Point in
The Ravens of the Storm. And how magical this was, this
feeling of seeing the things you read about were real, this
having things you'd only taken on trust appear to you so
solidly, as proof of themselves, confirmed as true in front
of your own eyes.

*

Sitting on the cool, wet pebbles close to the waves' edge,
Peter was aware the tide was coming in and that Agnes
next to him was shivering – it being afternoon or later, and
she wearing only that strappy top and floaty skirt of hers.
Worried for her physical comfort, as any normal decent
man would be given this scenario, Peter would gladly have
stripped off his kaftan to offer her an extra layer. And yet,
having nothing underneath but pasty skin and a teenage
nipple piercing (which he'd been proud of up until today,
when somehow everything had changed with him and he'd
come to see the nipple ring as trite and false and try-hard)
he worried he might seem too forward. Because wasn't it
a bit much, really, to strip off a shirt that had been next

to your bare skin and to offer that shirt along with your semi-naked self like that to a woman you'd really in actual terms only met just a few hours back, even if she kept insisting it felt as if you'd known each other years?

But maybe they did have a connection – maybe she was right – and also, come to think of it, being older than him as she was, she'd definitely have encountered a fair few male torsos in her time, some of which must surely have been less impressive than his. Oh, but what if she laughed? What if she looked at him askance and then laughed? What if the now genuinely quite cold breeze turned his already pale and papery skin to mottled, pock-marked gooseflesh and his nipples stood erect and she laughed all the more at just how much scale had built up around her eyes that she had failed to see him immediately for what he really was – just a loser, a drop-out, someone to feel sorry for who didn't actually understand astrology at all because he'd been brought up just down the road in Hastings, which despite the coastal setting could not be more different from Japan or California, could not be more unaware and obtuse about the spiritual core of the Universe if it really, really tried – if it went and did a doctorate in being unaware and obtuse.

Watching the sun's last rays stretch over the wide horizon, Peter thought about multistorey car parks, about dead pets buried at night in their estate's communal garden. He remembered screaming in the foyers of multiplex cinemas until his teeth hurt, because what did an under ten-year-old like him care that popcorn was extortionate? He remembered Bernard Matthews' chicken nuggets, mumps, being sick on sticky lino floors, and berry-flavoured Lemsip. And somehow that woman from earlier drifted back into his head again, that sad mother, over by the shore.

Agnes stood up and lifted her eyes to the horizon. 'I always think they look like spirits,' she said. 'Ghosts passing to and from another world.'

What? Peter nearly said, but then remembered their deep connection and kept his mouth shut lest he should undermine it. They stayed in silence a moment longer, the waves creeping up closer to their toes. Peter started to regret leaving his flip-flops behind, all the way back in his booth.

'The gulls,' said Agnes. 'Don't you think? Like spirits.'

Obese scavengers of bins, thought Peter, shameless dive-bombers of helpless tourists' chips, shrieking in the mornings like just so many harpies, then shitting on you as you walk to work.

'Mm,' he said. 'Like spirits.'

Agnes, still-shivering, rubbed her hands over her bare arms. He should do something, he knew. He got to his feet.

'Let me walk you home,' he said. 'Before you freeze.'

'Home?' she said. 'Already?'

'Or somewhere else?' he said, praying she wouldn't

invite herself back to his, with its carpet of pizza boxes and mouldering mugs and the single armchair dragged right up to the TV because the wire on his Nintendo controller wasn't long enough to reach anywhere else.

'No,' she laughed, 'home sounds just great. Or my hotel room does, at least.'

'Where are you staying?'

'Just up the beach.'

'Nice?'

She shrugged, as if to indicate just how far material things such as the niceness or otherwise of a hotel room were beneath her. 'I'd say so.'

'Come on,' said Peter. 'I'll walk you.'

'You don't have to do that.'

'I want to, though.'

'OK,' she said. And to his most severe surprise she stretched up on her tiptoes and kissed him on the cheek.

*

As Alfie walked out along the sea defences, the world around him seemed ghostly. Not just ghostly out to sea but behind him too, where there were no people and no shops or roads or homes or anything, just half-built new villa-looking houses with identical balconies and big hoardings up with photographs of what they would look like when complete.

He imagined what it might be like to live in one of those houses, and to be here in Brighton all the time. Him and Mum – and Wallace, too. Maybe Wallace would find a new job here and they could sit on the beach on the weekends and pretend to be on holiday. Mum might get in better practice then, get better at being a holiday type of person and let the headaches go away, and Wallace wouldn't be so sad if he had a job again, maybe, although in truth Alfie didn't know exactly what it was that made Wallace so sad. He just was, and had been for such a long time now, though when Mum had first brought him to the flat he'd had longer hair and worn a nice blue jacket and had smiled really properly when Mum had held his hand. Alfie would suggest it to them later when he went back. Although wouldn't they be upset with him, for running off like this? Wouldn't they be furious? Probably, probably they would.

He sat down on the concrete and stared out to the ocean. Flecks of spray. A pair of seagulls fighting in mid-air with shrieks and beaks and beating wings and talons everywhere, and the last red rays of sunset behind them. He was feeling a little chilly now, but in a bracing way, the cold air luxurious after all that sun and running.

He took off his shoes and socks and rolled up his trousers to the knee. Coolness on his calves – and on his bare feet! Alfie never had bare feet. Mum worried so much about ticks and red ants and about sharp things in the grass or lurking hidden around bus seats . . . and yet, oh, but how beautiful the ocean looked, surging there below him. Element of mermaids, pirates, shipwrecks, pearl-divers and pearls, of octopi and coral reefs, and maybe even hidden cities like Atlantis. It was a different world in there, he knew, alternative to Mastercards and headaches. He wanted to go back to Mum and Wallace now and show them this, explain to them. Maybe then they would see too, and everything would be OK.

Where have you been? Mum would say, looking very angry when he approached.

I walked out on the sea wall, Alfie would say. *And I saw a mermaid.*

You didn't see a mermaid, Wallace would cut in, then. *Impossible. Mermaids aren't real.*

I know, Alfie would say. *I know that's what they've told you, but you shouldn't trust all the things they say. Because I just saw one, just here, just now – over by the wall.*

Which wall is that? Mum would ask. *How far away? You must remember, Alfie, love, I'm not as young as other mums, maybe, and you can't behave like this. It's just too much.*

I'm sorry, Mum, he'd say. *But you have to understand, I saw a mermaid. Isn't that a thing to celebrate? And anyway, you're young and beautiful, just like a raven-haired princess.*

Alfie, love, my hair is grey, she'd say, and look so sad. And Alfie, knowing that at not-nearly-yet-eleven he was out of his depth, would look to Wallace for some idea of what to do to cheer her up, only to see him staying thick-jawed and silent.

Except it probably wouldn't go like that, Alfie knew, because they might be angrier at him than that. Mum hated having Alfie out of her sight just normally, never mind almost after dark like this.

He stretched out where he was sitting, arching his back and yawning, enjoying the roughness of the concrete on his fingers and the coursing of potential strength through his arms – just waiting, like a stretched elastic band. He could do anything, right now. If a pirate ship pulled into harbour he could slaughter all the crew in hectic improvised sword-play – him against the many. He would liberate the jewels and gold and give it all to charity, except some he'd keep for him and Mum and Wallace, so they could come on holiday more often. Because, now, in the freshness of the wind and the spray he realised he loved being on holiday. Perhaps most of all like this, alone, the sea like a magic door or threshold he just had to cross to find another place where the things to be afraid of were clear, monstrous things you could face down with weapons and with shouting and heroic resolution, like magic beasts or evil armies. He would be much more suited to a life like that, he considered, than the one he had been allocated here.

And with one last faint whisper of regret about Miss Lennox, Alfie pushed off with his elasticated arms and launched himself like a gull – like a kite, like a rock someone else was skimming – off the wall and into the waves.

*

Peter ran down into the sea in what he hoped was an at least halfway convincing attempt at a spontaneous outpouring of *joie de vivre*. At some indeterminate point during their conversation, looking at Agnes had started to feel difficult, somehow, as they wandered along the beach towards the white cliffs, towards where apparently her bed-and-breakfast was. Maybe after she had kissed him on the cheek back there, that could have been the stage at which the easy, luxuriant atmosphere that had flowed around the two of them the whole afternoon had started to become rougher and colder, somehow more demanding. Probably, though, that was just the sea. Peter had always been very sensitive to changes in the mood and character of the ocean. That was something people had remarked on, even back in Hastings.

He waded out up to his knees, then tried to kick the waves kind-of-viciously, but the water only softened his movements and made them fluid so that instead of the bitter splash he'd imagined he kicked his leg like a man swimming, diving down below the surface, perhaps, to collect some hidden, buried treasure.

'Tougher than you look,' said Agnes, just a little way behind him.

She'd followed him out into the water, god knows why.

'Excuse me?' said Peter.

'It's so cold,' she said.

He looked down at his submerged feet and calves, blurry through the seawater murk and the evening half-light, then out along the beach. No one else was swimming, now. Or no human beings, only dogs. Most people were packed up and gone. All that hecticness and laughing and easy money and ice cream tidied away and only a very few stragglers left: locals, mostly, food vendors packing up their stalls for the night. He preferred it like this, really. All those happy tourists gone and the place his again. He turned back to look at Agnes. She was making a show of staring dreamily out into the sunset, but really she was shivering and looked a little pale.

'Sorry,' he said. 'I got distracted. Let's get you home.'

She grinned. 'That's OK,' she said. 'I like my men a little crazy.'

He took her hand and led her back on to the dry sand, which felt almost warm to him now, on his freezing, aching feet.

*

He was in the water. He was in the sea! But why had he done that? How could he have jumped off the wall? Mum would be furious, and Wallace – Wallace would pinch the bridge of his nose and go red like he did whenever things got really bad, like his head was a kettle or something about to explode with the nose-pinching the only thing keeping it in – and he'd back Mum up on everything and for once he'd be right, because even Alfie could see, this time, just how bad this was, this thing that he'd done. To jump in still almost fully dressed, and in his special new holiday clothes, too, which he knew for a fact had cost more than they could reasonably afford because he'd heard Mum say so to Sandra on the phone when she'd thought he was off in his room, and now look, he'd been wilful and so, so disobedient and ruined both shirt and trousers! And that was sadly certain because he could feel them, heavy with water, dragging around in the icy waves and trying their absolute best, it felt like, to tug him this way and that so that he had to really paddle, really kick, really fight to keep himself away from the concrete sea wall, which somehow looked so much more vast and solid from this perspec-

38

tive than it had felt when he was sitting on it. *No* – Alfie struggled, remembering the 2.5 swimming lessons he'd had before Mum had put a stop to him going in the water – *no*, he would not be dashed against the concrete defences mere seconds after finally jumping into the sea.

He kicked and he flailed and he scooped huge hand-fuls of the water, pressing his fingers together in the way that he remembered the instructor – James, his name had been, a university student who always wore green – in the way he remembered James telling him to do, so that his hands were like paddles churning, shifting water back and around like on those boats he had seen in that film – which film was it? With the people in clogs and that girl who had cried on the mountain . . . But his brain wouldn't work now, it wouldn't remember. The sea was too much, it was too strong. The waves were so horribly difficult to anticipate, often coming up much higher than he expected, so that whenever he tried to propel himself upward in the water, craning his neck to breathe, he got mouthfuls of seawater instead of air – or a mouthful of half-air half-seawater so that he still breathed it in instead of spitting it out like with pure seawater, and choked. What could have possessed him to jump, here, like this? It was so obviously the wrong and the stupid thing to do and yet he had done it anyway. Like running away along the beach, like screaming and bursting into tears at Imogen's birthday, like trying to make Mum breakfast in bed and smashing the milk bottle instead.

Taking advantage of a moment of the water being sucked out from under him and out to sea, Alfie gulped in a huge, salty, spray-flecked mouthful of air, and then throughout the next one, two, three, four waves that engulfed him he worked quickly underwater, scrambling at buttons and zips and tugging at the shirt and trousers, which seemed somehow both clinging and vast.

Finally he pulled himself free, letting the tide whip them away, and when he kicked his legs again, swimming back up towards the sunlight, it was a million times easier. *Hallelujah!* Then, using his newfound weightlessness and the fresh freedom of his uncovered limbs, he swam, he swam, he swam away from the sea wall, pitching all the might of his ten-year-old body against that of the waves. How good it was to feel strong, beating his own path through the tide, blowing out bubbles in huge, reckless bursts of underwater air and opening his salt-stung eyes to watch them. How good it was to feel this powerful and somehow . . . somehow *coherent*, like a shoal of fish, his whole body streamlined, licked over by water and united in this one enterprise of pushing forward, out towards the sunset, out to sea . . . And his ear was fine, his ear felt perfect, *he* felt perfect! Or at least he would have done, if it hadn't been so incredibly cold.

He stopped moving forward (though it had become much easier, much less effort the further he'd got from the wall) and began to tread water, propelling himself round to see how far he'd managed to come. There were the cliffs, there were those lines of ghost-ridden half-built identical houses, and there was the sea wall, further away than Alfie had expected – much further away, in fact. But he shouldn't have stopped swimming, probably, because his fingers and toes were suddenly so cold that it hurt to move them, and that was no good because he was far away, now, so far away from Mum and the shore and from anywhere he could be helped and healed and made warm again, and god, what was that? *Cramp*, in his left foot! Like a sea giant's hand reaching up from the deep and gripping, squeezing and grinding all the bones together until he surprised himself by beginning to scream.

*

It would have all been fine, Peter reflected as he walked back into town along the seafront by the side of the white cliffs, if he wasn't such a good-for-nothing loser who wouldn't know what to do with a beautiful woman if she literally threw herself at him – which was what had happened, actually, pretty much, back at the doorway of Agnes' B&B before he'd pushed her away and told her it was all a huge mistake. Why had he done that? (*Because you're a deadbeat with a talent for self-sabotage – you never grab the good stuff, son, you just let it slip by.*) And when had he last slept with a woman, even kissed a woman, or held a woman's hand that he could be so picky about Agnes?

He walked until he started coming up towards that slick new marina village they were building out here by the cliffs, and just the sight of its gleaming surfaces up ahead was almost enough to repel him back down the path. He carried on, dragging his feet for a while until he found himself walking at a pace so slow it was barely worth walking at all, so he stopped where he was and stared out to the ocean.

Sea foam. He loved sea foam. It was kind of like frothed milk. That same excitement, that same sense of wholesome fun. He yawned and then crouched down to rub some warmth back into his sore, freezing feet. Though it was dusk and everything shadowed, he could see they were completely white with chalk from the cliffs, like the feet of a man made of plaster. What was that song his mother had used to sing? So long ago, in the evenings, while she was drying her hair. *She passed the salley gardens with little snow-white feet.* He'd always pictured the girl in that song as being made from plaster too, an indoor statue put outside in a garden.

Would she have understood, his mother? Would she

have understood why, on arriving at Agnes' B&B to discover that instead of the Californian villa he'd pictured, it was dingy and remote, basically just two or three rooms in a streaked, dirty prefab way out of town – actually closer to the care-in-the-community homes and the caravan park than the actual city – why, on being confronted by Agnes' almost eerily reflective eyes as she threw her wrinkled arms around him and invited him in – actually invited him into that miserable, damp sinkhole of a building – he'd realised he'd wanted no part in it, no part in it at all, and had unwrapped Agnes' arms from his neck and said in tones surely as polite as anyone could ask, given the circumstances, 'Don't you think I'm a little young for you, Agnes?'

But no, of course she'd never have understood that last part. She'd been kind, his mother, which was a far cry from what it seemed he was, today. Still, she was long gone now and it was pointless to speculate. And there was nothing at all left he could do about how upset Agnes had looked except get well away and stay away so she'd never have to see his miserable face again.

It was getting dark now, fast. And he was cold and wished he had his flip-flops, or no, forget his flip-flops, he wished he had some proper, substantial clothing. He stopped staring and started walking again, up the path to the marina. *These houses*, he thought as he walked through their hollow ranks, and these advertising hoardings, with their gruesome blown-up images of fake families eating apples in pinewood kitchens and going sailing in co-ordinated knitwear. Who in the real world has a happy, smiling family like that? Like that beautiful, airbrushed wife, for instance, beaming at her Ken doll of a husband across the breakfast table as if he'd just that minute said something both insightful and hilarious? Did they seriously not realise how stupid it looked – whoever was building this place? And didn't they question the morality of it? The way these adverts played on people's yearnings just to make a quick buck? At least, Peter considered, he wasn't quite as disingenuous or contemptible as whatever cretin had made those hoardings. (*Though that cretin made some cash out of it, I'll bet, son,* said his father's voice in his head again, *which is more than you've ever done.*)

'Oh, Dad,' said Peter, out to the waves. 'I would honestly rather be penniless.'

But what was that, there, out in the ocean? The semi-darkness made it difficult to see, but it was something odd, certainly, something that was disturbing the smooth vista of the evening in a particular way that registered as trouble somewhere deep in Peter's gut. Was it a seal? Some kind of bird? Or . . . someone swimming. It was someone swimming. Maybe not even swimming, exactly. It was difficult to see from this far away, in the dusk, with the water dark and shifting, but, jogging out now down the length of the sea wall, Peter wished it wasn't so deserted here in this part of town – or even that he hadn't looked, hadn't seen. He wished that he'd been more of a man and stayed with Agnes in that awful prefab, if only to avoid this, this thing happening to him now.

※

He didn't know what would happen next, Alfie realised. He didn't know at all, when all his life knowing what would happen next had seemed to come quite naturally to him – whether it was sitting on the bus to school, knowing which lessons were in store for that day, or being back on the way home again, knowing what was for dinner, or even predicting exactly the way Mum would react when he told her something. He could, in fact, only think of one single time before this in his whole life when he hadn't known what was coming next, just those few days after his father had left . . . Oh, but then he didn't want to think about that ever, ever again, and especially not now, when he was finding it so difficult even to breathe.

The cramp in his foot had subsided at last but it had taken too much energy and strength of will to fight it, to move and uncurl his poor frozen foot in the water, and then the other thing was that he hadn't really been able to swim at all while doing it – just treading water with his other foot and his hands had been struggle enough – and as a result he'd been pushed even further away from the sea wall and the cliffs and the shore. Somehow the direction of the tide was different out here and he didn't understand it. He'd kind of assumed while swimming before that the tide and the waves would carry him irrevocably back towards the wall and that that was the danger. He hadn't even considered that a small person like him would be able to get so far out and cover such distance when normally covering distance was effort, not accident.

Although, wasn't it really, after all – now that the cramp was fully gone – was it not actually strangely kind of *beautiful*? With the water dark now like cold tea and the big sky with stars above him like something from that musical they'd seen with Max and Sandra that time, the one from Bollywood where in the ending everybody danced – and he could see the moon, a gibbous moon, they'd learnt in Geography, and it really seemed, now that he stared at it from this angle, that the moon was spherical. Which of course it was – Alfie knew that. It was just that he'd never quite *felt* it like this before; he had never *felt* the moon was spherical.

He stretched his limbs out in the churning, rocking waves and relaxed, letting himself be tossed like a doll, like a branch, like some driftwood. The gleaming water over his bare skin was beautiful and the sky was beautiful, the moon was beautiful, and he was a part of it all. It could even be a kind of magic, this thing that he was feeling now: this overwhelming beauty, this sense of unity in all the things around him. Maybe this was it, his big adventure. Maybe this was . . . But then what was that? That figure in the distance. That figure waving from the end of the sea defences.

Curiosity made Alfie put some effort back into his limbs. He spat out a mouthful of seawater and hauled himself upright again in the waves so he could see the shore more clearly. But who *was* that, on the wall? Waving, waving. Alfie raised a hand above the waves as far as he was able and waved back. It seemed after all like it might be rude not to, like refusing to shake an adult's hand at a party or not saying *thank you for having me* after going to play at Robin's house – but who *was* that? He was only a small sketchy figure in the distance, about as high from this far off as the very top of Alfie's thumb on his waving hand, and yet Alfie had seen him somewhere before, he was certain. Oh, if only his eyes weren't so blurred and stung from salt water. Blue clothes, long hair, pale skin . . . and then he understood. And he realised that though he'd always hoped for something like this he'd never fully *expected* it, because it was just too wonderful a thing, too improbable and too much like something from some marvellous book to have a place among the everyday happenings of his own life. And yet there he was: the wizard, from earlier, on the beach. And surely it was now – surely this was the way they were really meant to meet. It did feel more appropriate, after all, with the glittered sky and the peril of the sea and no other people about to get in the way – just the two of them waving and calling to each other, over all this distance. Maybe this was what happened next, then. Maybe magic. Maybe wizards.

'Help!' shouted Alfie, as best as he could while choking on seawater. 'Help me!'

*

At the end of the wall now, psyching himself up to jump in. Peter knew how to swim, but honestly? He hadn't been in the water in ages. Which might seem ridiculous, seeing as he lived right next to the ocean, but then you never do make the most of the things on your doorstep, as people said. And though he'd always prided himself on having something of an affinity with the waves, it was definitely more of an abstract thing, more metaphorical, like the way he asked sceptics to receive interpretations of star charts, and faced with this situation now, he couldn't help but be afraid that were he to jump in after that man – or that kid, as it looked like, that *kid*! – it would only get them both in deeper trouble.

But that kid . . . He was so far away it was almost impossible to see anything about him clearly, so probably it was just some kind of paranoia that was making him think this, but didn't that kid look familiar? Especially now he was shouting and waving his arms in the moonlight, pale as it was. Surely that was the kid from the beach, earlier? The one who'd been rude to him about his kaftan. Except actually, now Peter thought about it, the kid hadn't been *rude*, exactly, had he? He'd asked him if he was a wizard, which was, all things considered, very different from being rude. In fact, in kid terms being a wizard was cool, being a wizard was great. So this kid had come up to Peter, filled with innocent, joyous excitement, and then bam! Peter had spat it back in his face, had sworn at him, even. Oh, but the kid was still there in the ocean, still struggling. This kid he had snubbed and cold-shouldered already . . .

Then it occurred to him. He saw it quite clearly. He saw why he had sworn at the kid on the beach, why he'd pushed Agnes away, quite roughly and literally when she'd tried to kiss him, and why, even, he'd failed to do anything more impressive with his life than run a little fortune-telling hut on Brighton beach. It was all for this, this meant-to-be moment. The planets decreed it. He was *meant* to be walking down this very part of the coast at this exact moment when this kid, this kid who he *owed*, needed that karmic repayment the most. It made perfect sense. This was his chance – he could feel it – his chance to make amends. He stripped off his kaftan and found that he was shaking uncontrollably. He just needed a minute, that was all, to prepare himself for the coldness of the water.

*

In the ending everybody danced – the phrase kept turning round and around in Alfie's head like a planet in the dark, like the screensaver on Mum's computer, like the mobile he remembered now of rabbits spinning up above his cot when he was very young.

In the ending everybody danced.

He didn't even remember the name of the musical, the one they had seen that time with Max and Sandra, where in the ending everybody danced. He barely even remembered the dancing – just the fact of it; he remembered the fact of the dancing, at the end. And it was such a good idea, he thought, to have dancing at the end. Why didn't people do that more? Why didn't everyone have dancing? Everything ending in joyful harmony, all the characters clapping and laughing together, even the villains and the ones who'd been killed in the earlier parts of the story. But he was flagging again, letting his limbs slow down in their thrashing fight to keep his body from being covered up with water.

And this was no good, he knew. He was very young and this was not his time to die. Just like if things were different and he'd been a cancer child, having to fight to stay alive until he was old enough to use the magic powers that would save him. The same thing here, the same thing now. The sky could look as drastic as it liked, coming at him on all sides while he was tossed like this by the waves, and his body could feel as nauseated and frozen and beaten up as it pleased, but he had to hang on. He had to keep fighting just long enough so that the wizard could rescue him and bring him his destiny, deliver him to the next phase of his life . . . Oh, but his chest hurt, he couldn't say how much, and –

In the ending everybody danced.

– it would be fine to relax a little, now, surely? To stop battling so much against the pain. How long, after all, did he have left to keep on before the man on the wall came to get him? He felt his numbed limbs go slack again while the force of the waves – so much stronger than a not-even-yet-eleven-year-old boy; how could he ever have thought he could match them? – cruelly picked him up and tossed him, back and forth, up and under. Adventures often involved times of hardship, Alfie knew, but this was too much. Where was the wizard? Surely it had to be now? Or soon it would be too late.

Desperate to see just how far away the man was and how much longer he had left to wait, Alfie put one last almighty effort into his near-frozen joints and forced his head back up above the water. He saw, at first, only darkness and more sea and sky seeming endless in every direction, and he panicked a little. But then he remembered himself and fought against the tide, twisting in the water until he saw the white cliffs and the sea wall . . . and then there was the man. Alfie's wizard. He was still there. Not even casting spells or shouting or even waving like before, but simply kneeling at the concrete's edge. He was without his robes now, Alfie saw, the bare skin of his bent back so very pale in the moonlight. All at once Alfie realised he had never seen anyone look quite so unwizard-like, crouched like that all alone in the dark, head fallen into hands, shoulders shaking, maybe weeping.

And what was left to do? What was left to do now that this unthinkable was happening? Now that his hoped-for rescuer looked so helpless? No more special than anyone, no more special than even meat-handed Wallace, no stronger or more capable than a child.

In the ending everybody danced.

Stars danced too, a little, when seen from this perspective, rocking and tossing in the waves. *No, I'm not a fucking wizard*, the man had said. So there'd been no trick and no joke. He'd been telling the truth, and maybe that's what Alfie had run from really, back on the beach, and not from Mum at all. Poor Mum. What would she say? She'd be so disappointed. And so sad. She'd be so very, very sad . . .

– everybody danced

. . . and then there was Mum, sitting on the blanket with her lemon sorbet and trying so hard to have fun on the beach for him even though he knew, really he knew, how she would be so much happier at home with her feet up and the telly on and a mug of tea in her hand instead of all this sun and sand and pretending to be a holiday person. Mum, who he'd run from without excuse or explanation, assuming he'd have the chance to go back. Just Mum. His mother.

Finding a will in his limbs he hadn't suspected was there, Alfie started to kick, to thrash with his arms, and to swim – beginning on the dark distance back to the sea wall where the pale figure still remained, hunched and crying in the moonlight.

Bear

I found myself steering the conversation towards furniture ever more frequently. This question of how we would furnish our new house seemed an easy thing for the two of us to discuss, and now that we were spending so much more time together, shared interests that kept the conversation flowing felt important to cultivate. It was probably these long discussions of ours concerning our future furniture that led to me driving us to a small coastal town one Tuesday morning in May, to attend an auction of second-hand household items.

I think I imagined that we might visit plenty of such auctions in our time as newlyweds, and that this specific one might be unremarkable, in simply being the first of many. I'm not sure I had many hopes or expectations about what the morning might entail. Only, perhaps, that we might come away with a new sofa, so that we would be able to sit together in comfort during our evenings in the living room, instead of always facing across from each other on the upright dining chairs until it was time to go to bed. But if we didn't find that sofa at this particular auction, I reasoned, that was all right. We'd have plenty of time to find the right one.

A few unremarkable ornaments and picture frames were brought out before us, none of which my wife or I ventured to bid for. Then the auctioneer's assistant wheeled out a silver trolley, on which was balanced a bear. I say *bear* – clearly it wasn't a real bear, come to terrorise the meagre population of this small English town. It wasn't even a taxidermy bear. I only hesitate to use the word *teddy* because although that would aptly capture his button eyes and furry coat and his too-small, stitched-in mouth, it would also belie the full extent of the bear, which was considerable. It was as big as me, more or less. Not quite in terms of height, perhaps, but what it lacked in stature it made up for in girth. If, for instance, someone were to chop me in half at the waist and then set the pieces side by side, that would give you some idea of the overall mass and scale of the bear.

I almost laughed aloud in the hush of the auction room as this ridiculous creature was put before the crowd. It seemed absurd – this bear, appearing in this context – a scenario so perfectly attuned to causing merriment that I wondered if the auctioneer had meant it for a joke. And yet no one else in that room seemed to share my amusement. Not even my wife, whom I had thought, up until that moment, had the same sense of humour as I did, exactly. We had laughed together so very often in those heady, hectic days before our wedding.

And so I felt obliged to suppress the smile I felt playing on my lips at the appearance of this giant creature. Everybody else around me – the auctioneer and my wife included – was simply watching it in perfect quiet, with expressions that varied from impatience to unconcealed boredom.

'One bear,' the auctioneer said. 'Stuffed, soft, in fair-to-good condition. Slight wear on the upper right shoulder, stitching a little frayed on the right leg. Going for fifteen pounds.'

I looked behind me, turning in my seat to survey the hall and see which of these small-town people might go so far as to bid for such a monstrous thing. Their expressions, however, remained as listless as ever.

'No one? No one at all? Not one amongst you who would bid fifteen pounds for such a magnificent bear as this?' The auctioneer's voice echoed in the hall. 'Twelve pounds, then. For twelve pounds. Giant stuffed bear, going for twelve pounds.'

I craned around in my seat again to study the hall behind me, feeling sure some poor soul would respond to this new starting price. It was just too awkward, seeing that creature slumped there, brought before us on its trolley, heavy head lolling and limbs akimbo. Surely someone would crack?

And then I felt movement in the chair beside me, and my wife was raising her hand.

'For twelve pounds, yes, that lady in the blue.'

I turned to my wife, expecting her to smile, to show some sign that she, too, had seen the grotesque comedy of the bear, and that this bid of hers was a kind of prank. She looked, though, as serious as I've ever known my wife to look, her grey eyes flitting back and forth between the auctioneer and the bear itself, her hand still raised.

'Going to the lady in blue for twelve pounds.'

I didn't understand what was happening. We'd come here for furniture – for useful things to fill our home. This bear was vast, impractical, ridiculous. It wasn't at all the sort of thing we wanted. But then, thank god, unexpected blessing, here was another woman – not my wife – here, in fact, were two other women, one at the back of the hall and one at the front, also raising their hands to make known that they were willing to pay for and take home this bear. Both of these women were, like my wife, over thirty but under fifty. Neither was particularly glamorous. One of them wore a hat. My wife turned to me at that point, her eyes sparkling.

'Should I do it?' she said. 'I'm going to do it. I'm going to win this one – you'll see.'

I didn't respond in any way. I was too taken aback. The auctioneer called twenty pounds, and my wife raised her hand. Then she raised it again at twenty-five, she raised it at thirty, she raised it at thirty-five. And yet the other women proved reluctant to yield. I stared at my wife, trying to catch her eye, to signal something of my apprehension, but her gaze was fixed forward, intent on the auctioneer. Forty. Forty-five. Fifty. We by no means had money to burn, being comparatively young and so very new to married life, and yet still my wife raised up her hand – steady, reliable, her grey eyes clear and watching the auctioneer with quiet resolution. Fifty-five. Sixty. Sixty-five. Eventually the other two women became intimidated by the strength of feeling that flowed between my wife and the bear, growing stronger with every number uttered by the auctioneer. For a moment I was almost proud of her, even if it did mean we had to bring back this vast sixty-five-pound bear, to share our home with us.

I tried my best to accommodate the bear into our lives, and for a while it wasn't too difficult. We put him in the second bedroom, and since I almost never found myself in there I rarely saw him. I noticed, though, that my wife sometimes went to check on him, popping her head into that room after breakfast, or excusing herself from the dining table in the hours after supper (we still hadn't found ourselves a sofa; our appetite for auctions had vanished as quickly as it had appeared). She'd go up and sit with him as he sprawled on the bed, his sagging body filling the small mattress. I started to suspect she was tucking him into the covers at night.

One Saturday morning in July, when we were sitting on our dining chairs with the newspapers spread out on the table before us, coffee brewing in the pot and all the windows open on the airless summer day, she said: 'Darling, I've been thinking. I would like to see how the bear fits in a different place, if that's quite OK with you. It just doesn't feel right – don't you agree – to have him shut away in that little room where you never seem to go?'

It seemed innocuous enough, this idea of hers. We had plenty of space, after all. I agreed, and that very day the bear came out to join us in the rest of the house.

She tried him in the living room, where he sat in the corner, lolling next to a vase of dahlias and watching us as we sat at the table and talked in the evenings. It seemed a perfectly fine arrangement to me at first – only a little eccentric, if we were to have visitors round. As the long summer days wore on, though, and the bear continued to sit in his corner – my wife often changing the flowers next to him, or rearranging his limbs from day to day – I became aware that somehow, I was starting to become inexplicably impatient with everything and everyone, particularly when I was at home. I snapped at my wife when she spilt gravy on the table cover, and then when one of my shoelaces broke I swore so loudly the glass seemed to rattle in the windowpanes.

At first I thought it must be the summer weather that was doing it, the gruelling lack of rain that was turning all the grass to straw and sending mosquitoes whining around our room at night. That is, until one morning when I looked up from my newspaper to face the round, glassy eyes of the bear – his smiling face flopping to one side as he watched us at the table – and I began to suspect that this new feeling I had was nothing to do with the weather at all.

When my wife came home from work that evening she found me sitting cross-legged on the floor (we still didn't yet own a rug) opposite the bear, studying him with close attention. I had been trying to figure out just what it was that so disturbed me about him, and was in the process of forming a hypothesis relating to his superfluity, to the fact I simply couldn't understand how such a thing as he could ever reasonably be wanted or loved by anyone, in any context.

The scale of him meant he would be useless as a sweet animal that might have sat in the corner of a child's bed in a possible vision of the future, to be cuddled and petted while the child's parents told the story of how the bear came to be brought into their home by the child's mother, and of her steady resolve and enviable nerve at the auction house. And then the bear-ness of the bear – that is to say, his large, beaded eyes and tight, woven mouth – rendered him uncomfortable to use as, say, a beanbag or a futon, or a huge throw cushion for napping upon casually, as who could nap casually upon a thing like that? A thing with a look in its eye that you would feel upon you as you lounged and dozed. I didn't know what my wife might feel about it, but I wouldn't feel comfortable at all.

My wife flitted over to kiss the crown of my head when she saw me like that, sitting with the bear. And for a moment I thought that perhaps since I'd figured out something of what was troubling me about him, things might get easier again. That we'd laugh together like we'd used to do in the weeks after we'd first met, when I'd take her out to dinner, and then sometimes we'd go dancing.

'Darling,' she said, then. 'How funny you look, the two of you there like that. I've been wondering, in fact, if you think he might like a change of scene. He must get so bored, just seeing the same thing day after day.'

So she took the bear to sit in our bedroom, talking to him as she moved him, saying things like, 'That's it, dear, a change is as good as a rest, you know,' as she hefted him up the stairs, her slim arms wrapped around the girth of his waist.

And that was where the bear stayed, all throughout

those airless summer nights, his drooping head and flopping limbs propped up against our bedroom wall. Over time, I couldn't help but feel that his presence there disrupted my ability to conduct sexual relations with my wife. My wife had never been an overly demonstrative sort of a woman. Not for her were the moans and cries and hair-pulls of the less subtle forms of erotic fantasy. Before the appearance of the bear, in fact, it had been our natural pattern for her to lie still on the coverlet, watching with her small, grey eyes while I tried a variety of ways in which to excite her. And I feel sure that she enjoyed this approach of ours, because afterwards she would always, without fail, enfold me in her arms, holding my head to her breasts and stroking my hair as if to say, *Well done, you poor, mad boy, well done.* I felt ushered in, during moments of this sort. Sheltered. As if nothing in the world could do me lasting harm. With the bear in the room, though, I found it difficult to attain and to sustain the required levels of arousal. Probably, I know, it was unmanly of me to be put off by the presence of an inanimate thing, to be so unable to provide my wife with the satisfaction she deserved, simply because there was another face in the room, belonging to neither her nor me.

In any case, my wife began to sense the difference in my manner. She may always have been relatively quiet in the past, but I'd understood that she was far from unobservant. It was obvious, then, that she noticed this new discomfort of mine, or at least that she noticed the decline in the quality of my efforts to impress her. No longer did she cradle me at the end of our lovemaking; no longer was I afforded that brief moment of peace, that safety in the feeling that I was a person who was loved. Instead, after labouring and sweating and getting almost nowhere, I would lie next to her – the two of us there, side by side like dominoes – and I'd look over at the bear.

What was it about his presence that caused me such profound difficulties? It couldn't simply be my dislike of his fundamental uselessness. I even forced myself to consider, during one of those too-hot summer nights, lying next to my silent wife, whether I was somehow *jealous* of the bear? And yet, as I stared hard at his woven, smiling snout and at the worn-out stitching on his shoulder, I simply couldn't understand how such a pointless creature could provoke such a passionate emotion.

It wasn't until the next morning – as my wife was pouring out the coffee and smoothing back my hair with an expression almost like concern – that I realised precisely what it was about the bear that truly troubled me. I nearly pushed my chair back from the table then, when it hit me – nearly walked straight out of our kitchen without explanation, leaving her to have her breakfast on her own. I took a quick sip of coffee to cover my alarm.

But could it really be – I wondered to myself that

morning, as we sat opposite each other, buttering toast, passing the milk jug, trading sections of the paper as if nothing were at all amiss – that my wife saw very well the awkwardness of the bear? That she was, in fact, keenly aware of his internal incompatibilities, of the way that he could never be a creature of real worth, and that this was precisely what drew her to the bear, what had made her bid for him in the first place? What if, indeed, my wife was one of those women who took a shine to lost and pointless things: to things that were not broken *per se* but that rather had some flaw to their design or manufacture, meaning that they'd come into the world not fit for any purpose, destined from the first to be entirely valueless? Was it possible that she was one of those people who actually felt sorry for lost causes of this sort? Who loved them, even, for the very reason of their pointlessness, perhaps because she knew that if she were not the one to do so, then absolutely no one would. I had never noticed this tendency in my wife's character before, but then why would I have done, when the only other thing before the bear that I'd been aware of my wife loving (aside from her family, who, of course, she'd been given at birth, with no real choice about whether to love or not) was me?

That thought returned an awful lot in the days that followed that revelation over breakfast, particularly in the evenings, when my wife and I lay side by side, the bear looming over us in the same way a crucifixion scene looms above the pews inside a Catholic church. So often did I worry about it, in fact – so much did I fear what the true nature of my wife's love might be, and what might really have inspired that tenderness I had felt in her arms as she'd held me in the days before the bear – that I stopped being able to sleep at night. Instead, while my wife slept, I stared up at the bear, making myself more tired and doubtful and irritable with every hour that passed, and becoming less and less able to discern anything about myself a sane, right-thinking person could possibly find to love.

At last, when it had chewed me up so much that I was turned into a wreck, I just asked my wife, straight out, 'Why do you love that bear so much?'

'Oh,' she said – and her eyes almost lit up in the way they used to, in those early days back in the spring – 'it's just a silly thing, really. Don't laugh when I say this, darling, please. You have to promise not to laugh or think I'm being crazy, but I suppose that I just feel a kind of kinship with him. A certain sympathy. Sometimes I just can't help but feel a little like the bear. Does that sound ridiculous? Really, I'm afraid it must.'

She was smiling, but the thought that in any of the days we'd shared together I'd let her feel that way – that she was something like the bear – that I'd allowed that to happen, unchecked and unnoticed, without even suspecting it might be how things were with her, even for a moment . . . it overwhelmed me to realise it. I had thought I understood pretty well the way she thought and felt, and I had hoped that our life together, though admittedly imperfect, was still on track to grow into something shared and seamless and miraculous.

She reached for my hand then, my wife. Her eyes were still laughing in that way I hadn't seen for months, as if it had been a relief to her to finally articulate her thoughts about the bear. I thought perhaps I should apologise to her, or at least try to put into words the awful problem of the distance I'd suddenly seen stretching between us. And yet I found I couldn't – I found I couldn't even speak. So I simply caught her hand instead, and held it for a moment.

The Rat Catcher I

I was called to the palace a few days after the new king was crowned. I supposed it was a sign of the new regime, this cracking down on vermin. I just hoped it was only within the palace walls that the king was wanting to exterminate rodent-kind. He'd have had a hard job of it out in the city proper, after all, given the ferocity of the latest infestation, and then of course I'd have been out of a job if ever he succeeded.

I'll tell you a secret. Even then, I'd never much liked the palace. It seemed an obvious architectural monstrosity, for one thing, with all those flourishes and archways and columns and gargoyles. On top of that there was the simple, galling fact of such a large and lavish building being allowed to stand so useless, for scarcely anybody actually lived there any more, so far as I could tell. It seemed that practically only the new king was left, rattling around up there all on his own, the ranks of the old dynasty and its attendant hangers-on having faded into ludicrous paltriness. Still, I don't deny I was a little curious, getting to poke around inside the grand old royal residence like that. I even thought it might be a nice break from my work in the city, which had been getting ever more intense as the infestation escalated – rats in every gutter, rats in every kitchen, rats prancing round people's ankles in the streets, spoiling food, scaring housewives, mauling infants, spreading sickness.

I was met at the door – the servants' door obviously; even I don't flatter myself I'm grand enough for that ghastly main entrance – by an old woman, all bent over as if she were so used to bowing and scraping she'd simply decided to stay that way to save herself the bother of straightening up to her full height. She looked precarious and I'll admit I was alarmed. I am, you understand, very much of the opinion that balance in a posture is a most important thing. This lady who received me, however, seemed to have adapted herself to a hunched kind of existence, or at any rate she didn't fall as she shut the door behind me and handed me a ring of keys – a reduced copy of the set, I supposed, that she wore at her own waist, though she didn't look like much of a housekeeper. That done, still wordless, still not even looking at me properly, she shuffled away down a dark corridor to my left. I'll admit that I expected something more of a welcome. A few words of greeting, perhaps. Maybe even the offer of a tour around the property – for the purposes of showing me the identified locations of rodent activity, of course. Still, a man like me is quite accustomed to making his own way, if nothing else. I decided there would be no point trying to follow her, and slipped the keys into my pocket, setting off to explore.

Most of the first rooms I came across seemed shut up and empty, no sign of anyone having so much as stepped inside them for a matter of years, which was much as I had expected. Perhaps more surprisingly, though, I also found plenty of evidence to indicate a healthy, even thriving, rodent community. I somehow managed not to see any actual rats during those first explorations of mine, but there wasn't a curtain about that hadn't been gnawed, and some of the dustsheets even had nests in them. It wasn't long before I found the kitchens – which, incidentally, didn't look as though anything much had been cooked in them for months – and these kitchens, let me tell you, were a celebration, a cacophony, of all things rat. A shrine to dear old *Rattus rattus*, with droppings and scratchings and teeth marks in abundance.

And yet even here, while I could hear them snaffling and running about in the walls, I still couldn't see them. My theory is that rats all over this city have learnt to avoid me. I imagine them talking about me in the cellars and gutters, sitting up on their haunches and twitching their ears as tales of my victories are spread far and wide. A local legend, that's me. Quite the phenomenon, if you ask in the right circles.

I reached into a bag of maggoty flour and scattered a handful over a few dusty surfaces, then I turned my back and stepped out into the corridor. I whistled a tune as I waited, then took the watch from my pocket to count the second hand around for another minute until it was time to return to the kitchen again. And when I did, I discovered almost everything exactly as I'd predicted. The flour, that is, was now imprinted with hundreds of ratty paw-prints – just as I'd suspected it would be – but the size of them, my god! It was like nothing I'd seen before in the whole of my extensive career. It was almost majestic. The creatures I would be dealing with here, it seemed, were rodents fit for a king.

I reached into the recesses of my coat for my rat-catching gloves, and also for a little tin of one of my favourite concoctions. A modified version of solanine, some might call it, but I prefer Emerald Dust, on account of its being bright green. These people with a technical name for every small thing in the world – no poetry in their hearts, I tell you. I took a moment to admire the proportions of my fingers once the gloves were on, holding my hands up to the dim light of the one narrow window near the ceiling, then I added just a pinch of Emerald Dust to the paw-printed flour, mingling it in with the tips of my fingers to make the green less lurid.

Rats are more or less colour-blind so it wasn't for them that I went to the trouble. I just hate messy work, and I've always been that way. With just one day in that old house-keeper's shoes, for instance, I'd have got the whole palace sparkling again – or maybe two days, on account of the apparent lack of staff. It was odd. I hadn't expected it to be bustling, exactly, but it did seem just a little too deserted to be quite correct. Still, at least that meant there would be no one to complain about the traps and poisons I'd be putting down. A definite mercy, that, for if those footprints were anything to go by these specimens would be far too large for my more discreet methods. The poison I'd laid in the kitchen, for instance, would likely be only enough to do away with one or two of them, possibly even only slow them down, the size to which it seemed they'd grown. That was fine, though. At this stage in the game I only needed them to lie there and still be waiting when I got back so that I could take a good long look at them. I'm like a tailor, you see: I need to see my victims before I work so that I can devise exactly the right end for them – engineer the perfect fit.

Leaving such potential fun and games behind me, I turned down the corridor and up a stone staircase. Soon enough I'd found my way through a mouldering door, which I suppose must have once been green baize, and stepped into some kind of drawing room. At first it seemed an awful lot more luxurious than the servants' part of the house where I'd been wandering before, and much more the sort of thing you'd expect to encounter in a royal palace. But I only had to look around a moment and to advance a few steps before I was aware of that stale scent in the air again, and of teeth marks on the wooden feet of furniture, holes in the skirting boards, and long scratches down the heavy velvet curtains.

I didn't notice these things, however, quite upon the instant of coming into the room for two good reasons. First, the curtains were drawn, everything illuminated by low lamplight and firelight, which was a little disconcerting considering it was a bright morning outside. Secondly, there was a girl in the room. She was facing away from me and staring into a mirror – turning herself about in it, this way and that – and I could see immediately from the style of her dress and from the shine of the candlelight on her hair that this was not the sort of person with whom I was used to conversing. I saw too, then, that her beauty was not the kind that could survive even a day in the harshness and dirt of the city outside. And yet still I could not help but stay and watch as she lifted a paintbrush from her dressing table, and carefully dabbed it to her face, minutely altering the curve of an eyebrow.

'Are you going to tell me who you are?' she said. 'Or do you plan on simply standing there for the rest of the morning?'

I looked around the room. 'Me, Your Highness? Is it me you're talking to?'

'Don't call me that,' she said. 'My name, as you well know, is Ethel.'

'Ethel,' I repeated, relishing the sound of her name in the tones of my own voice.

'Ye-es,' she said. 'Goodness, you're not the brightest of souls, really, are you?' She turned to look at me and I saw her face, then, for the first time the right way round, not in the mirror. 'And really,' she continued, 'you'd do well to think a little more before you ask people foolish questions like that. Who else, indeed, could I be talking to?'

'Perhaps,' I said, 'perhaps to your reflection, Miss Ethel.'

She laughed at that. She had a low, musical laugh – pitched lower than you might expect from the look of her – and with a nice edge to it, like she was a girl who knew what she was about. I took off my gloves and folded them into my pocket.

'Or to the rodents in the walls,' she said. 'In any case, do come and stand a little closer. Come where I can see you.'

I stepped further into the firelight.

'Come on, yes, that's it. I don't bite, you know. There's really no need to be frightened.'

'I'm not frightened, milady,' I said.

'Milady,' she repeated back at me. 'Now there's really no need for any of that. As I told you, Ethel will do just fine . . . Oh, but you're older than I thought you were.'

'Sorry, miss – Miss Ethel.'

'There's no need to apologise,' she said. 'There's nothing you can do about something like that, I'm sure. But what was it you said you did here? I'm afraid I've quite forgotten.'

'I didn't say,' I said.

'Oh,' she said. 'How mysterious of you.'

I found it difficult to hold her gaze, then, so I stepped away, towards the windows.

'Why shut yourself up like this?' I lifted a curtain to let in some daylight, and felt mould and dust transfer on to my hand as I did so. 'You should go out, meet some people, have an adventure or two. There's nothing like it, I promise you. Good for the blood.'

'I wasn't in the mood for sunlight today,' she said, but she came and stood next to me all the same. Up close like that I could see all the particles of powder on the skin of her cheeks and the shining grease of the paint around her green eyes – imperfections that only made me like her more, somehow. Still, I didn't want to stare, so I turned to the window and together we looked out over the grounds, at all that frozen empty space. There was a thin trail of smoke curling out of the trees ahead, and she sensed my question before I could ask it.

'He lives out there now,' she said. 'My brother. With his dog. Ever since the night of the coronation. I don't think he likes it in here with us ghosts very much.'

'Your brother?' I asked.

She nodded, a shadow passing over her expression. 'Yes,' she said. 'Or my half-brother, at least. I'm the elder. And certainly more like our father, if he'd ever cared to see it. It's funny, on days like this I still can't quite believe he's gone, our father. Do you know he's still upstairs?'

We carried on looking out the window while I turned over what she might have meant by that.

'Still upstairs?' I asked eventually.

She reached up and touched my arm, the one holding the curtain open, a signal, it seemed, for me to let it fall again. The room slipped back into gloom.

'You'll see,' she said, with a strange kind of smile. And then she went back to her mirror, leaving me with a sense of being dismissed.

'Is there anything I can do to help you, Miss Ethel?' I asked.

She shook her head. 'That's quite enough for today.'

And yet, as I nodded and bowed my way from the room, I couldn't help but wonder: if that was quite enough for *today*, then surely that begged the question, what about tomorrow?

*

The second most interesting development of that first trip to the palace occurred in the afternoon when I returned to the kitchen to find something waiting for me, courtesy of the Emerald Dust – or two things, in fact – lying unconscious on the stove-top. I stood back to make my professional assessment: size of a small house cat; snout elongated to more than average proportions to accommodate a vicious set of fangs; spooling pink tail; enormously fat – how did they get so fat when there was no obvious food source about? – scabby fur; tiny red eyes. I breathed out, one sigh of admiration before I got on with the job in hand, chucking them into a sack and slinging them over my shoulder. I'd be taking these devils home for inspection.

And yet I spent the best part of the next hour wandering the halls, searching for the old housekeeper, perhaps – anyone from whom I might take my leave. It didn't seem right simply to pack up and go back to my workshop. Not when I'd been sent for personally, after all – asked for, almost – by the king himself. Everyone, though, seemed to have vanished into the walls, or disappeared, silent, behind locked doors. At last I made my way down through the snow of the palace drive, eyeing that curl of smoke from amid the trees and wondering why on earth our new king chose to spend his days shut out in the forest like that, and how much he could possibly see from there of what was afoot in his household.

*

I live in a part of the city seldom frequented by the more genteel elements of society: the abandoned factory district. It's the legacy of a moment of hopeful stupidity on the part of the old king a few years before I was born, when he thought it might be a good place for making steel and went ahead and built four factories in what was then wasteland to the east. They opened to huge fanfare and excitement, I am assured, and the steel business lasted all of five years. These days, they're home to a bunch of strays. A bunch of strays and me. And it pays not to be too squeamish about rats, I've found. I've a whole attic – the uppermost floor of an enormous steelworks – all to myself. I have my own workshop for building my traps, a small laboratory for my poisons and tinctures and powders, a dressing room, even. And, oh my lord, the view is beautiful. Or at least, I don't know if *beautiful* is quite the word where this city is concerned, but for a man like me, born and bred here, I assure you it takes my breath away. I can climb out on to the roof from the windows and see the whole metropolis stretched out before me, those hundreds of buildings – white, or grey, or black, depending on how filthy they are – and the crows: dark wings everywhere, like the shadows of angels.

When I arrived back on that particular rat-catching day, the sack containing the two palace beasts over my shoulder, I found myself appreciating my rooms to a greater extent than usual. I supposed it must have been something to do with having had the opportunity of comparing them to the residence of a king, only to find I liked my own home far better, and I laughed aloud at that idea as I settled back into my humble, orderly home again. I ran my fingers over my workbench, with its neat lines of hammers and nails and pliers and saws and sandpaper, all stacked up in a most orderly arrangement. I surveyed the corner that served as my sleeping area, and continued to feel so glad and so confident, so cheerful at being home, until I looked over towards the mirror and I found my mood turning almost melancholy to think that I was the only person there to appreciate all that perfection. Just myself and the rats. An enviable party.

I unloaded the beasts on to my workbench with some difficulty, as one of them had been sick in the bag and was already looking as if it were shaking off its dose of the poison. Evidently I'd need to work on a stronger formulation of the Emerald Dust before I returned to the palace. I swiftly injected the creature with the hypodermic I always kept ready for just those occasions, then set to work on the business of devising a trap.

It's not as simple a process as you might suppose. There's an art to it, definitely – both from the point of view of basic engineering, and, shall we say, from a more psychological perspective – and I've always taken a certain amount of pride in it. Each of my traps, for instance, includes a version of my signature: that is, the last thing the animal sees before it dies will be the image of a starlit sky, because to my mind at least there's nothing with more poetry in it than a living soul being reminded of the immense possibilities and scope of the universe, just in the moment before leaving it.

I got out my ruler and callipers and began measuring up the two creatures, and I worked long into the evening, until the last light from the windows had faded and I was forced to look up from my bench to close the curtains, and light the lamps. Something distracted me as I did so – just a thought, a sensation of fingers brushing my arm – and even though I knew I was running out of time if I wanted to snatch a few hours of sleep before dawn, I took a moment to make something else before settling properly back into work. Just a little star, carved out of wood. It was only a very small thing, and harmless enough, I thought.

*

I carried my new trap to the palace bright and early the next day, under a cloth, so as not to alarm the good citizens of the city as they went about their morning business. I still had the keys in my pocket so I let myself in – the servants' door again, of course – and made my way to the kitchen. I didn't go in, though, not immediately, because I realised the old housekeeper was in there, talking to somebody. I leant my head slightly past the edge of the doorframe to see who she could be conversing with . . . and that was part of the mystery solved: how the rats had managed to make themselves so fat. She was hunched over in a little chair by the stove, hands full of grain, and with a whole litany of the cat-sized rats at her feet, eating from her fingers and climbing over her legs and ankles as she reached into the recesses of her dress for more feed. There was no one else in there with her; it was the rats she was talking to, calling them pretty names and singing out-of-tune snatches of lullabies. I am not a squeamish man but something in my stomach turned over at the sight. The rats were one thing, but it's not like they could help their being rats. I have never, though, felt quite so much revulsion towards another human being.

I swallowed the bile in my throat and, leaving my trap in the corridor outside, I stepped into the room. The beasts scattered from her feet as I did so, disappearing into dark corners and cupboards and through holes in the walls. The housekeeper jumped back in her chair, as if somehow that could shelter her.

'You should wash your hands,' I told her. 'And learn to sit up straight. It's disgusting, the way you hunch over all the time. Like an animal.'

'Please,' she said, eyes watery, mouth slack, 'there's so little life here, in this place.'

She spread her palms wide, as if that might explain. My stomach lurched again, nothing to do with the rodents this time.

'I was sent for by the king,' I told her. 'And if you can count on one thing, it is that I will do my job well.'

At first she said nothing, just gaped her fishy mouth at me, dribbling all down her chin.

'You are a cruel, cruel man,' she stammered out eventually.

'You disgust me,' was all I said before I turned and left the kitchen, picked up my trap again, and took myself off to a less repulsive part of the palace. I felt I needed an antidote.

*

I found Miss Ethel in a room on the third floor. She had her back to me, looking out of a tall window, her dark hair loose and flowing over her shoulders. I peeled off my gloves and put down my machine, still under its cloth, in the centre of the floor. It was a strange room, like a room for a child but nearly bare – just a fireplace and an old wooden rocking horse shoved up by the wall, its bright paint all chipped. The walls were in a similar state of disrepair, with their patchy peeling plasterwork, but it looked as if they had once been painted with images of animals and strange creatures. What could have been a winged lion stood out to me on one of them, and as I ran my fingers over it some of the plaster came away in my hand – a broken bit of wing.

'This used to be the nursery,' Ethel said, still at the window. 'I hated it in here. I wanted to be with my father in the throne room, sitting at his side as he once promised me I would. That promise, though, was made back in the days before he was married and my brother was born. I used to stand here like this every day, looking out. I'd never move, from hour to hour, and so gradually they took the toys away. There was no point to them, you see, if I never played with them.' She turned round to look at me. 'Do you enjoy games, Mr Rat Catcher?'

'How did you find out who I was?'

'Oh,' she said, 'my mother told me.'

A horrible thought occurred to me then, but I did my best to dismiss it outright.

'I'm afraid it's not a pretty profession,' I said.

Ethel merely nodded, and then walked over to my machine. 'What's this? Some novel instrument of death?'

'I wouldn't touch that.' I hurried to her side but she'd already pulled off the cloth. Her eyes widened as it settled around her feet.

'What do you think?' I asked her.

'It's—'

I don't know what I expected. *Savage. Cruel. Ungodly.* But she never finished the sentence.

'How does it work?' she said instead. 'Show me.'

'Are you sure?'

She nodded.

I'd never shown a trap of mine to anyone before. Not because they're secret or anything. Only because, well, it's not often anyone's interested. And I did wonder if it was quite the appropriate thing to be sharing with a lovely young woman like Ethel, but then I had an idea she wasn't the kind to be easily shocked. I got to my hands and knees on the floor by the trap.

'Regardless of the direction from which the victim approaches,' I told her, 'he will see one of these wooden gangways leading him up on to the main structure of the machine. He'll follow it up, spiralling, thus, until he reaches this curtained platform at the top here, at which point he will pass through the curtain and fall . . . into this chamber here,' I tapped the wood from the outside, 'whereupon—'

'Wait,' she interrupted. 'How can you be so sure the creatures will behave as you say they will? How do you know they will run up the ramps?'

'Ah,' I smiled. 'An excellent question. I have impregnated the wood with two of my special scented powders, only faintly at the bottom of the ramp, but to a rat's nose getting stronger all the time as we progress upwards, coming to a head, the strongest intensity, just behind the curtain.'

I've never seen anyone look quite so transfixed. Inwardly I congratulated myself on my powers of explanation.

'Would you like to look behind it?' I asked, stretching a finger out to push the little velvet curtain to one side.

She stepped closer and looked through. 'Oh!' She sounded surprised. 'Why is it all filled with stars? It looks like midnight.'

'That? That's my signature,' I told her.

'Your signature?'

'What else do you see in there?' I asked her.

She looked again. 'A blade,' she said, 'hanging from the ceiling.'

'Yes. And?'

'A . . . door.'

'Indeed. A door that can only be opened from the inside.'

'Why include something like that?' she asked.

'To let the rats out, of course.'

'I thought this was meant to be a trap.'

'It is, believe me. The blade is poisoned. Coated with a dose of my Emerald Dust.'

I let the curtain fall and showed her the tin containing the new, especially lethal batch I'd made in the early hours of the morning. She reached for it then, but I slipped it back into my pocket before she could touch it. I turned back to the trap.

'The mechanism causing the blade to swing is triggered by the weight of the falling rat. There's no way for him to escape getting sliced, but if he happens to be roughly the size and shape of the two creatures I found in the kitchens yesterday he should only pick up a slight graze. He might not even realise he's been injured. He can leave through the door at the bottom, but he won't get far before the poison kicks in.'

She breathed in, looked up at me.

'A trap you don't even have to empty,' I told her.

'Scented powders,' she said, her face suddenly very hard to read.

'I'm sorry, milady?'

'You mentioned scented powders. Just now. But my nose can barely detect them. What are they scented with?'

'Ah,' I smiled. 'Now that's the fun part. You've got to think like a rat – figure out what they want, what they'll chase.'

'Food?'

'Yes, always. But in a place like this, where there seems to be sustenance in such abundance, we might need a little sprinkle of something else to lure them up the ramps. Something even more irresistible.'

She was watching me carefully now.

'Can you guess?' I asked her.

'I couldn't possibly say,' she replied, but she was lying, I could tell.

'The smell of female rat,' I told her anyway.

'That's why you said *he*,' she said.

'That's why I said *he*. I'll make another one for the female rats all in good time, but just this once I didn't think it would be polite to do ladies first.'

'Quite,' she said. 'It's certainly impressive. I suppose one could even call it . . . well –' her green eyes flickered up to meet mine – 'I suppose one could even call it beautiful,' she said.

Beautiful. The word seemed to expand and brighten in the air between us, like an ink blot in a bowl of water. I studied her for a moment, then reached deep into my coat, feeling amid the tins of powders and the bottles for the smooth points of the wooden star I'd carved the previous night. I held it out to her in my open palm but she flinched away from me.

'Take it,' I told her. 'It's for you.'

She frowned down at it. 'Like your signature,' she said.

'I suppose so. But, please, I know it isn't much, but I've never shown a trap of mine to anyone before. Not like this. I'd like for you to have it.'

She raised her painted eyebrows at me, took a step closer, then snatched it out of my hand, quick as anything.

'An honour, Miss Ethel,' I told her.

And then everything was spoilt by an abrasive clattering from the door. It was the old woman bearing a tea tray. I found that after what I'd seen her up to that morning I couldn't even bear to look at her, so I went off and stared out the window instead.

'I thought you might like some refreshment,' I heard her croak behind me. 'Anyone would need a quick break every now and then from such –' and here I heard a small crash as she put the tea tray down on the floor – 'strenuous work.'

I remained by the window, listening to the old woman and Ethel unloading and ordering the tea things – just a lot of clattering and rattling of silver spoons and sugar tongs on china, neither of them needing to talk or comment upon the process at all, apparently. It seemed, indeed, quite the practised ritual for the two of them, and I couldn't help the horrible suspicion I'd had earlier creeping back into my brain.

'Will you not take a cup with us, Mr Rat Catcher?' Ethel asked, quite casually.

'No, thank you,' I told her.

The thought of Ethel drinking the old crone's tea made me sick to my stomach.

*

I managed to shake off my foul mood as I went about my work in the rest of the palace, until I was feeling more jovial than I had done in weeks – daydreaming alternately about Ethel, and about lacing the old witch's tea with Emerald Dust. Lurid green the poison may be when in its powdered form, but a dark blend of tea – a good Assam, perhaps, or a Lapsang Souchong – would hide its colour nicely, I was sure. It was funny, I didn't even know if it tasted of anything. I'd never been in a situation in which it had mattered before. Not that it mattered now, I was very quick to remind myself. But it was an interesting point to consider.

To take my mind away from such morbid thoughts, I let myself wonder what it might be like to show Ethel round my apartments. It tickled me to imagine her there, all her refinement and poise displaced like that into the world of everyday things. And yet my home was better kept than the mouldering palace, was it not? And she seemed to spend so much of her time here staring into mirrors or out of windows. Perhaps she would relish the opportunity to escape.

I pictured myself bowing to her, taking her hand, inviting her to spend an evening with me – or even to stay, perhaps, for an extended visit. Though my rooms as they were would probably be a little too stark and too bare for her tastes. I'd have to get her a dressing table, of course, together with any other small trinkets she might like to have about the place to feel quite at home. But the view over the city – she would like that just as it was, I had no doubt. I pictured myself stepping out of my window and reaching back to offer her my arm, so that she might follow me and climb out on to the roof herself. And we would stay like that for hours, in my imaginings, arm in arm, side by side, talking together about this and that, watching the dark birds as they circled the buildings before us. She was so happy in my company, in those daydreams of mine.

*

Again, I couldn't find anyone about that evening to dismiss me. The palace really did seem a miserably quiet and lonely place, especially after dark. Of course I didn't genuinely think of taking such a person as Miss Ethel back to my apartments with me, but as I roamed the halls, hallooing and whistling in the hope of finding some other living soul about, I couldn't help feeling even more certain that she must wish herself away from it sometimes. Surely such a bright young creature as she was must occasionally yearn for more and better company?

I was lost to considerations of this sort as I made my way home, crunching through the layer of fresh snow over the palace drive, and only momentarily roused from my ruminations by the sight of that smoke again, twisting up from the trees. That was another curious thing. The new king had ordered me here, yet since arriving I hadn't so much as clapped eyes on him. When would he emerge from the woods? Surely he must come to the palace sometimes, after all. He couldn't very well govern from out there, could he? I gave a quick bow to the smoke on my way past. Probably it was a foolish gesture, but it made me feel more cheerful, somehow, as if things were still in better order than perhaps they seemed.

Back at my lodgings for the night, I tugged a blanket around myself and made my way over to my workbench. I was weary and eager to escape the freezing air for the warmer world of sleep, but there was something I wanted to do first. There was still an offcut of wood left from when

I'd made my trap, and I worked at it then with saws and with sandpaper until my eyes were so weary I could barely make out anything any more in the dim light. At last I held what I'd made up to the window to check it met my satisfaction. A perfect crescent moon.

I gathered the blanket back round myself again and hobbled over to my mattress, my bones stiff with cold – and nothing, I tell you, not even a smile from Miss Ethel, could have been more pleasurable to me than it was to finally close my eyes, and surrender my mind to dreams.

*

I encountered no one in the servants' area of the house the next morning, not even the old housekeeper, which was something of a relief. The first living thing I came across was another of those vast rats, twitching on the countertop where I'd laid the Emerald Dust those two days previously. I pulled on my gloves to swiftly break its neck, then carried on through the gloomy corridors to the grander parts of the building.

I was making my way back to the old nursery when I heard that distinctive musical laugh of hers, coming from behind a door further up the corridor from me. It was standing ajar, which was why I was so bold as to push it open, and to step a little way inside.

I saw my mistake immediately. Ethel wasn't alone, you see. She was sitting before a mirror – just as grand and gilded as the last one I'd come across her looking into – and there was the old housekeeper behind her, comb in hand, plaiting her long dark hair. The crone didn't react to my sudden appearance in the doorway – probably she was too absorbed in her work to notice my reflection – but not so Miss Ethel. She stayed perfectly still under the housekeeper's hands – and how I hated to think of those filthy hands all over her shining hair – but her eyes flickered up straight away to meet mine in the glass. I took one last look at her, finding it difficult to bear how perfect she looked, there in the glow of the lamplight, and then stepped back out of the room, away from that nasty scene.

I was back on my way to the nursery when I heard a door shut behind me, and sharp footsteps echoing up the corridor.

'Mr Rat Catcher,' her voice rang out, 'surely you don't plan on leaving us so soon?'

'Miss Ethel,' I said, turning to tip her a nod. Her dress was green that morning, to match the colour of her eyes. 'I assumed you were busy.'

'I'm never busy,' she said. 'Who could be busy in a place like this?'

'But the housekeeper, milady.'

'She can wait,' said Ethel. 'In fact, I've been telling her all about your trap – the one you showed me the workings of yesterday.'

'You have?'

'Yes,' she said. 'And she was more interested than you might expect. Now come and sit by me, while I have my hair coiffured.'

'I'm afraid I shall have to decline, Your Highness.'

Ethel's expression clouded over. 'I've said this before, *Your Highness* is wrong. My name, as I have told you—'

'Is Miss Ethel, I know. But I must be on my way,' I told her. 'I have my work to attend to in the rest of the palace. King's orders, after all.' Given what I'd begun to suspect might be the horrible truth surrounding the mystery of her attachment to the old woman, I thought it best to refrain from expressing the disgust I felt at the prospect of spending even moments in her company.

'Oh, but surely we don't have quite so many rats as all that,' Ethel said.

I couldn't help but notice a false breeziness to her tone then, odd when she was usually so self-possessed. Surely she realised the true extent of the palace's vermin problem, living amidst it as she did?

'Quite enough to keep me busy, Miss Ethel,' I said.

Her expression hardened then. 'Very well,' she said, and turned to go.

'Miss Ethel!' I called after her.

'Yes, Mr Rat Catcher?'

'I have something for you.' I peeled off my gloves and rummaged in the pockets of my coat, finding the little crescent moon I'd whittled for her last night at my workbench before falling asleep.

'Here,' I said, offering it to her. 'To go with your star.'

She took it from my palm and studied it, seeming quite serious for a moment, turning it over in her fingers.

'Are you really quite sure you wouldn't like to join us?' she asked.

'Quite sure, Miss Ethel.'

'What a great shame,' she said. And then she slipped back into the room, and closed the door.

*

Could it really be true that someone like Ethel, someone so beautiful and elegant – and half-sister to the king, no less – counted it a *shame* that she wouldn't be spending the morning with me? I didn't let myself believe it at first.

As the morning wore on, though, my mood grew sunnier until I was feeling almost jaunty, recollecting the words *what a great shame*, as I laid my trails of Emerald Dust up and down the mouldering corridors, alternating the trails of green with lines of my scented powders, sprinkled there to act as bait. Again, I found myself whistling a tune as I worked. Just a sea shanty, picked up from some sailor or other from a job down at the docks, but the melody was pretty, and that morning it brought home to me how, even in the ugliest of situations, doing the ugliest work, there's always some beauty about if you know where to look for it. I wasn't even particularly unnerved when – while working in a new part of the palace, lacing the chewed-up fringes of some fancy tapestry with dustings of poison – a door creaked its way open and a young man I'd not seen before stepped out. He had excellent posture, I noticed, and was dressed in a clean, new-looking suit. Perhaps it was the contrast between his well-kept appearance and the rest of our surroundings – or perhaps it was his sour expression, or the way he closed his door behind him as if to shield whatever precious things might be in there from my vulgar, prying eyes – but I have to say I disliked him immediately.

'I would be much obliged,' he said, 'if you would stop making such a racket.'

'Me, sir?' I asked him, shaking the excess of the Emerald Dust from the fringing. 'Racket, sir?'

'Your whistling,' he said, 'is out of tune, and disturbing me in my work.'

'Oh, well then,' I said. 'In that case you must accept my sincerest apologies, my dear sir. I shall confess, indeed, I'm afraid I've never been known for being of a particularly musical inclination.'

'Evidently,' said the man. 'And I'd be grateful if you could pursue whatever it is you're doing elsewhere. I'm working through some most important documents and cannot afford to be distracted.'

'But I'm the rat catcher, sir,' I said, 'and I must follow my work wherever it takes me.'

He regarded me with something that looked a little like surprise, or perhaps it was simply disgust.

'I'm obliged to set my traps and poisons down in every corridor of this palace,' I continued. 'Royal orders.'

'Ah, so the king sent for you?' said the man, with a sigh. 'Well, there's a certain logic to that, I'll allow – a *rat catcher* – when seen from that perspective.' He took a moment to examine his fingernails. 'I'd be obliged to you in any case,' he said, 'if you would leave my room alone, at least. Oh, and I wouldn't touch the nursery, either. But you'll have figured that out already, I dare say, if you know what's good for you.'

'The nursery?' I began to ask, but he'd already slipped back into his room and closed the door.

I finished my work on the tapestry. Then, though, curious in spite of myself, I went over and studied the plate on his door. It had been polished up to a shine, taken proper care of in a way that was completely at odds with every-thing else I'd seen in the palace. And *Shaw, LLD*, it read, in fancy, curling script. I couldn't help myself – I spat on the ground right in front of it.

*

I know it was foolish of me to let a man like that ruin my afternoon, but I couldn't help myself turning over and over in my head what on earth he might have meant about leaving the nursery alone. I started to wonder, even, if it might have been some species of threat. His manner had been hostile enough, and though I could think of no clear reason why he should have taken so much against me simply for going about my appointed work, might he have been into the nursery and done something untoward to my trap? The idea preyed on my mind until I could no longer continue my work, and I dropped my scented powders and my tin of Emerald Dust right there where I was in the corridor, going back to check on things.

*

I found my trap apparently unharmed, standing exactly as I'd left it in the centre of the nursery floor – exactly as I'd left it, that is, except that now there was a scattering of dead rats all around it, spiralling out in a pattern of resilience, a map of which of them had been strongest, most able to run a distance from the blade before the poison overwhelmed them. Seeing those dark bodies laid out like that on the ground, I was reminded for a moment of crows, of the shadows their wings made on the rooftops as I watched them soar over the city from my window. Except this wasn't like that at all, really. In many ways it was the opposite of that kind of liberty, that kind of grace. I crouched down to look at the nearest dead rodent. Its eyes were bulging wide and I could see an icy damp-ness round its jaw from where it would have spent its last seconds on this earth foaming at the mouth. *One could even call it beautiful*, Ethel had said to me. To think I'd almost believed it.

'Don't touch it,' came Ethel's voice from the doorway behind me. I hadn't heard her approach, but did my best to show no surprise.

'It's all right, I'm used to it,' I said. 'It's dead already, there's no harm it can do. See?' I picked the rat up by the tail to show her, but regretted it instantly. She flinched and almost cried out, her hands flying to her mouth.

'Don't touch them, please,' she said. 'I'd prefer it if you didn't, really.'

'I'm only doing my job,' I said. 'Listen, Ethel, you haven't seen a man called Shaw around here, have you?

He told me something about the nursery, that I shouldn't do my work in here. Can you think why he would say that?'

She smiled a little, though she still looked very pale. 'That was sweet of him,' she said.

'Excuse me?'

She shook her head. 'It's not important.' She wandered over to the window and took a moment to look out at the frozen lawn. She seemed to be steadying herself after the shock I'd given her, taking slow, deliberate breaths and smoothing down the front of her skirt. Then she turned, a framed silhouette against the fading afternoon light. 'But I didn't come to look at corpses,' she said. 'I wanted to ask you, would you come for a walk with me? I always feel so lonely at this time of day.'

I could hardly believe it. I stood up from where I'd been crouched on the floor, next to my trap.

'A walk?' I asked.

She smiled. 'That's what I said.'

'The old woman too?'

'She doesn't have to come. In fact I think she'd rather not.'

'Are you sure?'

'Of course I'm sure,' she said. 'Why wouldn't I be?' And then she came over and took my hand. It should have been the most marvellous thing in the world, and yet it only made me cringe. I was still wearing my rat-catching gloves, you see, and heaven knew what rodent filth had got on them throughout the day that was now in contact with her smooth, perfumed skin. I tried to draw back but Ethel only gripped my fingers tighter, towing me along to the doorway.

'Come on,' she said. 'Don't be *shy*, Mr Rat Catcher – don't be *rude*. I know you want to come with me. I've found us a bottle of wine and everything. It'll be fun. Don't be such a *bore*.'

She was right, I did want to go with her. More than anything. And so I silenced my doubts and followed her, trying my best to believe that a king's daughter might really want to spend an evening with a man like myself. Perhaps it was true she was lonely.

*

We wandered together down the drive and through the palace grounds until we came to the lake, huge and iced-up, its surface glittering in the moonlight. She poured us out two glasses of wine, and we sat down on the bank, using my coat for a picnic blanket. I was freezing, but so happy I couldn't have cared less.

'My mother doesn't like you,' she said, out of nowhere.

'She is your mother, then?'

'Of course,' she said.

'You can tell her from me I'm not too fond of her, either.'

'Oh,' she took a sip of her wine, 'she's not so bad. You've probably seen the worst side of her.'

'Is that so?'

She thought for a moment. 'When I was a very young child,' she said, 'my father was so fond of me. I was his little bird – his nightingale – until of course he truly fell in love, and married. As you'd imagine, my existence became somewhat inconvenient to him then, and I was banished to the nursery. All those years I spent, shut up there as if my illegitimacy might be catching. And yet I was never quite abandoned, not completely, because of her, you see. No one ever asked her to, or ordered her to do it, but she was always there somewhere, watching over me.'

'Along with scores of vermin.'

Ethel didn't reply to that, only carried on sipping her wine, not looking at me. After a while she asked, 'You know . . . the way you build traps?'

'Yes,' I replied.

'Am I right in thinking that while all the doors and pulleys and ramps are very clever and everything, the real skill of it all –' she turned and met my eyes now – 'lies in figuring out just what your victim wants? What they need.'

'The lure,' I nodded. 'It's a savage business, really, when you look at it properly.'

She didn't reply and I noticed her green eyes were glittering more than usual.

'Ethel, are you crying?'

She shook her head and looked back out to the lake. It was a minute or two before she spoke again.

'What's my lure?' she said.

'I'm sorry?' I said, though I knew exactly what she meant.

'What do I want? What do I need?'

'I – couldn't say, I'm sure.'

'But you have thought about it.'

I considered trying to make her laugh, then, somehow, or to distract her with something flashy, or clever. But: 'Of course,' was all I said.

Suddenly I felt so ashamed of the way the long years in my profession had taught me to think. I stood up and walked the little way out to the edge of the lake to clear my head, half-hoping she might follow me, maybe even take hold of my hand. She didn't, so I joined her again after a few breaths. Her face looked strange in the moonlight. I wondered if she was cold.

'I wish it hadn't been you he'd sent for,' she said then. 'I wish it had been anyone else.'

'I'd take you away from here, if you'd let me,' I told her, speaking the words like a man in a dream. 'We could forget about this place – the king, the rats, your mother – and just go. You could come and live with me, if you liked. I could show you my workshop and the view from my window.'

She didn't say anything, didn't even look at me, only stared straight ahead, her face unmoving.

'You're being absurd,' she said at last. 'Sit back down and drink your wine.'

The two glasses were sitting side by side in the snow, hers empty, mine still nearly full. I drained it in one gulp before saying, 'You're cold. It was a stupid idea to sit outside on a night like this. Let me take you back to the palace.'

Standing up, she shook her head and pulled her fur coat tighter around herself. 'No, thank you,' she said. 'I can make my own way back. This is my home, after all.'

'Of course,' I said.

She reached down for my coat, brushed off the worst of the snow, and returned it to me.

And somehow then it felt important to explain to her what it really was that she meant to me – aside from all this talk of lures, and traps – and yet I hardly knew where to begin. 'Thank you,' I told her. 'Before you, you understand, there was no one else in this world who'd ever – no one who'd ever entertained the possibility . . .'

I stared out at the trees for a moment, trying to recover myself, and when I looked back at her she was watching me with something like pity in her eyes.

'Don't look at me like that,' I said. 'Ethel, don't – please don't look at me like that.'

I reached for her hand, but she only turned from me and ran away, straight across the snowy ground, back towards the palace.

'Goodnight,' I called after her, as she went.

I didn't have long to wonder about her strange behaviour. I hadn't even got as far as the palace gates before the muscle cramps started and I began finding it difficult to breathe. And as my limbs twitched and I convulsed over my lurching stomach, something clicked in my mind and I reached in my pocket for my tin of Emerald Dust. It wasn't there, of course. I could see it in my mind's eye, lying next to my gloves in the corridor where I'd dropped everything after letting the empty words of that lawyer get under my skin.

I fell to my knees, and as I did so I couldn't help but wonder if this wasn't something I'd brought on myself, stepping so far out of line as I had – oh, but then there was the thought of her eyes to contend with, and her smile – and I couldn't quite believe this was what I deserved because surely a world that had room in it for such beauty also had mercy in it, somewhere? And then if I hadn't been shaking so badly I could have laughed, because the very last thing I saw before slipping into unconsciousness was a vast open sky filled with stars.

Heart Problems

How many times can anyone pack and repack the same suitcase without feeling amazed, just amazed, that they still haven't made a decision yet about what to do, where to go, or whether, in fact, it is truly necessary for them to go anywhere at all? London is beginning to drive me mad, or at least to make me horribly unwell in some way I can't define, the feeling being too general to pinpoint precisely. The sheer volume of people is part of what's doing it. The battle of wills involved even to walk down a street, the physical proximity to strangers on a rush-hour tube – the woman next to you angry, shoving past, stony-faced, because a few minutes ago a tall man with a rucksack didn't notice he was leaning back into her, crushing her hand against the metallic yellow pole she was hanging on to just to stay upright – because it is always like this here: strangers being careless, even cruel for no reason other than it is so uncomfortable, so unpleasant to exist here in this city, only the fittest allowed to survive and all the elderly and children tidied into hospitals, nurseries, and goodness knows where else, conveniently out of sight.

So yes, you could say that I don't like it here, that I

don't like the pace of it, or how I fear it's changing me, and yet still I remain. I remain though I like it less and feel worse each day, and though I find myself constantly, now, turning over how disconcerting it was to go home to Killorglin last Christmas. I couldn't comprehend at first the time it took to have my passport checked at Kerry airport. I found myself frustrated that the woman at the desk seemed to know every single family passing through and to want an update on the smallest things – how John was getting on with his new bicycle, how Aoife's baby was and whether teething had got any easier, whether Fintan there was still allergic to dogs and how that was for Annie, having little Coco, as she did. And then there was the waiting in the newsagent's for Rory to hand over my twenty-pack of Marlboros, watching the slow dance of his old hands over the ancient 1990s cash register – and of course my sister's face as I lost patience with Dad, for taking so long to formulate a thought and then translate it into words. Dad, who seems to be slowing down as rapidly as I am speeding up, moving so slowly he's started going backwards, even – recent events vanishing in the fog as he reverses through time.

And yet, as I say, here I am: certainly not committed to being here, but not yet fully resolved to go, keeping my battered suitcase packed and ready in our too-large wardrobe, just in case something comes to me when I least expect it – some revelation, some magical solution to the problem of my life, which, as it stands, and as it has been standing for the past two hundred and fourteen days now, will not fit together into any kind of resolution. It's as if each of those days is an individual piece from a separate jigsaw puzzle and they're all jumbled together in a box, undecided as yet about the extent to which they'll ever be able to fit themselves together into a new completed picture.

On the days when my fiancée, Beatrice, is out at work, which is most days, even some Saturdays – she's very driven – I remove the suitcase from the too-large wardrobe (I say 'too-large' because it takes up half our bedroom, and is just obviously bigger than the scale of the life any reasonable kind of person would lead) and I spend twenty minutes or so looking over the contents. Sometimes I remove an item, and sometimes I add something that hadn't occurred to me as being necessary before. This morning, for instance, I added a compass, because it's always useful, I've decided, to know where you are in relation to something fixed, even if you are unsure of where you're going.

Some mornings I'll take every single item out of the suitcase, laying them out in a line on the bedcovers, and I'll handle each object in turn, checking each thing over carefully: *envelope of sterling, envelope of euros, keys to our London flat, keys to my family's house all the way back in*

Killorglin, woollen hat, my mother's copy of The Sea, The
Sea *(which still I haven't managed to find time to read),
emergency cigarettes* – and now – *compass*. Then when I've
completed my rounds I'll replace the objects in the case,
click the catches shut, and consider whether that morning
will be the morning I seize the suitcase by the handle and
step out of our flat with it, never to return again.

Perhaps I will find it in myself to set out through the
streets of London, gripping the peeling leather of the suitcase handle as I wind my way through the vast, polluted
city towards Liverpool Street Station, imagining that I'd be
home in time to help my mom and sister make the dinner,
in time for Dad to recognise me as the version of myself
he finds familiar, in time for long, discursive breakfasts,
for walking on the beach and for driving up into the
mountains, like we always used to do when my brother
and sister and I were small. Once at Liverpool Street, I'd
catch the train up to the airport, and once there, I'd walk
straight up to the Ryanair people and say, *One way to
Kerry, please, and I'll pay on card. No, I don't care how
much it is, because in this world there are more important
things sometimes.* Except inevitably, this being Kerry, I'd
be told by the smiling garish-yellow-and-blue-clad woman
on the desk, *We have no flights to Kerry today. You'll have
to wait till Wednesday* . . . and then somehow, though
Wednesday is not so long to wait – not so long at all con-

sidering the grand scheme of human life and geological time and the fact I've spent two hundred and fourteen days waiting here unsure already – the legitimising urgency, the romantic spontaneity of the moment will collapse, and my mind will drift back to Beatrice and our lovely London flat with all her tealights and her clothes and the crockery we bought together.

And it will seem simply unacceptable, simply too cruel to someone who obviously deserves far better, to plan in advance like that and book a flight for Wednesday and disappear while she's at work, having faith that I'll be there when she gets home to make risotto or bitch about the neighbours or whatever else she wants to do. And so I'll walk out of the airport – this parallel me in this purely hypothetical, speculative version of my life – and I'll step on to the train again, the suitcase getting heavier in my hand with every mile we cover and the compass needle inside spinning, pointing, swinging between the front door of our London flat and the direction of the airport, back the way I came.

I'd walk through the city's evening rush, then, dodging through the footsteps of hatchet-faced commuters (and how I wish I shared their certainty at wanting to go home) until I'm away from all the pavements and the buildings and I'm walking through Hyde Park. It'll be less crowded here, the impatient hordes replaced with a slightly more relaxed type of pedestrian: those who walk with purpose, still, but who also are determined not to let the city win, and who will look up, sometimes, to smell the roses. And I'll try to smell those roses too, and yet as I do I'll find that though I'm surrounded now by green, the path beneath my feet is still tarmac. And though Hyde Park would seem lovely, I am sure, to anybody passing through who is not in my condition (for condition it must be, though of what kind I cannot say) I feel only disconcerted, and almost even quite upset, to discover that in the heart of London's mayhem – piled-up buildings, tower blocks and offices and railway lines all jostling for prominence – there is only this artificial lake, these tarmac paths, these pigeons, this vast empty space.

I'd arrive back late, then – this hypothetically roving version of myself – but still in time to shut away the suit-case – so heavy, now, that I can hardly understand how I lifted it before – back into the too-large wardrobe, and then to wash my hands and face and comb my hair before I hear Beatrice – my fiancée, that is, her name is Beatrice – before I hear Beatrice's key turn in the lock.

'Hello, darling,' she'd say. 'Been out?'

'Only to Sainsbury's,' I'd say, returning her kiss hello.

'Get us anything for dinner?'

'No,' I'd tell her. 'No, I'm sorry. I forgot. I was looking for goat's cheese, but I couldn't find the one I like.'

'You never find the one you like,' says Beatrice, visibly annoyed – for why couldn't I have pulled myself together sufficiently to remember to buy groceries for dinner? I've had all day to do so, after all, while she's been working. I don't tell her that I feel like there is something very wrong with me – that my head hurts, my chest hurts, my gut hurts, that I am labouring under some kind of unidentified yet all-consuming sickness. I don't remind her that my grandparents used to run a dairy on the island where my granda grew up, where the goats ate only grass from his fields and my grandmother made her cheese infused with flecks of seaweed that her brother-in-law used to gather from the shore. So of course it's no wonder I can't find the one I like here, I will never find it, though that doesn't stop me looking. I certainly don't tell her about the suitcase, or the airport, or the spinning compass on the train.

I generally tell Beatrice I'm spending my days job-hunting. She always says that there's no hurry, and that she makes more than enough for the both of us for now, but I want to be able to contribute. She nods seriously and understandingly whenever I tell her this. Beatrice is one of those individuals who is consciously trying very hard to be a good person. Not that she isn't naturally a good person. It's just that she's always making such an effort at it, if you know what I mean.

'Of course,' she says to me whenever I tell her I want to start working too. 'Of course I understand.'

So I tell her I'm job-hunting, and it doesn't feel like a lie. More a simplification. Because what I'm doing, walking around these streets all day, tossing bits of stale bread to the birds in Hyde Park, looking in windows, picking up flyers –

STOP_MOTION:
A 21st Century Dance Odyssey by Wendell Brown

FAT CATS SHOULD NOT HAVE NINE LIVES: MAKE THE BANKERS PAY

space vs. inspace: photography of the new mind

Cleaner: reliable, punctual and discreet, £8.50 an hour, call 0784965263 for more info!

– it all feels like some kind of unnamed equivalent for job-hunting, if you know what I mean. As if I'm hunting for something here in this city, definitely, but what it is exactly, I'm not sure. I think I'll know it when I see it, but then I suppose so must most people with a feeling of searching for something, even the most misguided, or else they simply wouldn't bother at all.

So today, anyway, I did what I mostly always do, and wandered along the Thames and through Green Park to the newsstand by the gates on Piccadilly. It's still surprising to me, this lack of newsagents in London, and how the very few that still remain seem to rely on alcohol just to stay open. Anyway, this particular guy I go to, this guy with the stand I get my papers from in the mornings – he's a true cosmopolitan, selling newspapers from all over the world. I pick up a copy of the *Irish Times*, drop it on the counter in front of him, and – 'Just this, please,' I say (why is it I can't buy anything without prefacing my purchase with *just this*, or *just these*?) – and for a brief moment it feels almost like being home.

'Dan,' he cries, this news vendor, embarrassingly sure of my name where I can't seem to remember his. 'How've you been keeping?'

He asks me this every morning, though it can only ever have been twenty-four hours or so since I last saw him – less, sometimes, because I occasionally call by to say hi on my way home in the evenings.

'Not bad,' I tell him, scrabbling in my pockets for some cash.

'Not bad?' he roars. 'Not bad? On a beautiful day like this?'

I grin, find a five-pound note, hand it over.

'The *Irish Times*,' he says, as he sorts out my change, and then: 'I love Ireland,' he tells me, for what must be at least the seventy-eighth time, considering the number of mornings I've been in London and then subtracting the number of days I took to find him and his newsstand, and then also subtracting the Sundays when Beatrice is home and I don't go out, the few days when he didn't feel the need to tell me this, and, of course, the odd day I was sick, or too depressed for whatever reason to even begin to consider reading a paper.

It's a funny thing, but he reminds me in some way of my brother, this news vendor – my brother Ciaran, three years older than me and an academic in Dublin. The two men don't look all that much alike. Actually, they look almost nothing alike at all, seeing as Ciaran is, for one thing, several decades younger, but there's something about the manner, about the atmosphere this news vendor projects that never fails to put me in mind of him, somehow. Perhaps it's simply the set of his jaw, or the way that he uses his eyebrows a lot when he talks. It occurs only in flashes, but flashes that make me feel as if I've found my way back to the summer after the Leaving Cert, visiting Ciaran over at college when he'd only been away there a year or so, the two of us standing on O'Connell Street in the rain with him chomping on a Subway, telling some anecdote about a girl in one of his seminars while the 747 buses swoosh their ways through the puddles behind us.

'I love Ireland,' the news vendor says again, and I bump up my mental calculation to eighty-six to account for the mornings on which he may have repeated himself. But then: 'My son's over there,' he says to me for the very first time, today. 'In Dublin. He's a good boy, my son. Your lot better be looking after him.'

'I'm sure they are,' I tell him, though I have to say I'm hardly listening, because a part of me is caught up, for whatever reason, in contemplating goat's cheese once again, while most of the rest of me is still occupied with thoughts about my brother – not as he was when we were students, but rather as he was last Christmas, in the kitchen with our mother, pale-faced over his cup of tea, promising to be home more often in the spring so that he might help out with Dad. Ciaran taking her hand over the table-cover and telling her it wasn't far, it was no bother, just a short train ride away and he could even come up sometimes in the week if he had a morning when he didn't have to lecture.

'I do miss him,' says the news vendor, 'but he's only young – round about your age, I'd say – and you young people have to see a bit of the world, don't you? Explore a bit, live in different places. But he's a good boy. He'll come home and settle near his dad when he's ready.'

Near his dad. When he's ready. As if the link between the two of them feels so strong there's simply no fear of the danger that one or the other of them will drift away; as if they have all the time in the world. He hands me my change and I stow it randomly in my coat pockets, where likely I'll struggle to find it later; where probably a few of the smaller coins will fall through the holes in the stitching and float about in the lining. There must be so much small change that's fallen into this coat over the years: euros, sterling, dollars, even some Swedish Krona from that bizarre family holiday we took in Stockholm, way back when the coat was new. It's a miracle, really, that I'm not magnetic by now. Or perhaps I am magnetic. And maybe the readings from the compass in my suitcase will be distorted by this magnetic field of mine, by this disorienting influence created purely out of personal chaos and bad stitching. I pick up my *Irish Times* and scan my eyes over the headlines of all the different papers lavished over the front part of his stand . . .

Article 50 one year on: the Brexit clock that won't stop ticking

Less than a decade left to take control of climate change catastrophe

Parisian zoo evacuated after 50 baboons escape

'Cheers, Dan,' says the newspaper man. 'You take care of yourself now.'

And – strange, unwarranted, unprecedented thing in London – whether he actually does or not, it sounds as if he really means what he just said, that it wasn't just a simple pleasantry.

I find myself urgently wanting to grasp his hand and ask him something like: 'Do you ever get this overwhelming feeling of disintegration? As if the whole world is splitting off from itself, breaking up into individual satellites? And all the separate component parts of everything have given up on trying to co-operate, or cohere?'

Except when I open my mouth I hear my voice simply say, instead, 'Do you ever have the feeling you're in completely the wrong place?'

He looks at me a little funny at that, but he doesn't laugh or anything. He seems to think about the question.

'Not really,' he says eventually. 'And if I ever felt like that I don't suppose I'd stick around for very long, wherever I was.'

'Because I've been wondering,' I find myself continuing, 'if it isn't time for me to stop this thing I've been doing, of pretending to be a Londoner.'

'What makes you say you're pretending?' he asks.

'Well, you see, I've got this . . . I don't know. I've got this pain, right here – and I've been struggling to see things clearly.'

'Listen, mate, maybe you should see a doctor.'

'I'm fine,' I tell him. 'Just a rough day.' A rough two hundred and fourteen days.

'You'll be all right,' he tells me. 'Everything's getting better now, anyway. Spring's on the way, don't forget.'

Nodding my goodbyes, then, wandering on my way down Piccadilly, I did notice a new warmth to the sun as I looked up to see a few early shoots making themselves known on the spidery branches of the otherwise wintery trees. And I tucked my paper more firmly under my arm, crossed the road to avoid the worst of the tide of people moving towards the tube station, and felt distinctly lighter for a moment. Somewhat less distracted and a little more at home in my surroundings.

Except, just then, just as I was starting to feel better, the odd thing happened for the first time. At least, I think it happened then. I suppose I can't be fully certain, it being such a bizarre thing, and so fast that by the time I noticed it everything seemed normal once again. And then of course there was the fact I was taken off guard that first time – not expecting it or anything at all like it to occur – and also distracted by the unexpected sight of the new leaves and my resulting thoughts about the changing of the seasons and the passing of time. But I did feel distinctly, in the way that we, as humans, are programmed to *just know* when something is emphatically not right with our bodies, that something untoward occurred here. A sharp pain in the centre of my chest shooting down my left arm to my wrist . . . and then the quick scent of woodsmoke, though nothing nearby seemed to be burning, the touch of rain on my face, though the sky was perfectly clear, and the faint sound of waves all mixed up with the salty tang of the sea on my tongue . . .

Oh, I tried so hard to think nothing of it. I thought forcefully instead about how much the news vendor had cheered me up and how I should really ask his name again tomorrow and how maybe I should put more effort into having some of my own friends here in London instead of simply hanging out with Beatrice's because look what a difference even a simple conversation could make. I hummed out loud to myself as I came up here, to Hyde Park, picking up this bag of stale bread on the way from that market down by Costa Coffee, my idea being I'd relax here for a while, enjoy the sunshine, read the paper, feed the pigeons.

Before we moved here, Beatrice and I spent four years back in Dublin. We were a good match there, I think, having quite similar lives. I had a job back then, one I quite enjoyed – or didn't hate, in any case – and we had plenty of friends in the city. We laughed a lot and we didn't sleep much and we didn't think hard about the future – or I never did, anyway. We were always so busy, the kind of people who never have enough time. One sunny Saturday while shopping up near Grafton Street Bea found a poster that read *Work Hard, Play Hard, Be Kind*, and she liked it so much we bought it and put it up above our dining table.

It seems to me now that it captured how simple things felt in those days, how easy a well-lived life seemed to envision and sustain. I only very rarely found myself considering the merits of other, hypothetical lives in those days, and that kind of thinking was only ever a ludicrous, happy kind of daydreaming back then. The things I used to imagine for myself . . . they were all dreams so much more rooted in ideas of the future than of the past. I often imagined, for instance, that if I were granted just a fraction more breathing space in each day, just a few spare minutes not spent working for money or doing chores or entertaining friends, that I'd learn to dance, or to paint, or even that I'd write a novel.

But I apologise, that is probably beside the point. It is so difficult, though, to determine what is truly relevant and what is incidental. Because something out of all of this, I swear, must be the crux, the centrepiece, the cause and core of my condition. Something here must be the point. Otherwise how am I to work out what is wrong with me? For something surely is. Because it was when I was think-ing thoughts very much along the lines of everything I've just been telling you – though what these thoughts were I'm afraid I can't quite precisely say now – while feeding the birds just along from here, up the path, over there, the odd thing happened again. The thing that is really starting to worry me now that it has fully happened twice, and also . . . well. As I'm sitting here talking to you now I do have to admit I can tell something untoward is going on, starting in the centre of my chest and moving through my arms towards my fingers, progressing down my legs towards my toes. A feeling I'm suppressing, right this moment, as a person might suppress a yawn, or an urge to vomit. Probably it isn't much; probably isn't anything at all – I don't know that I'd be able to explain the problem if I went to a doctor, for instance – but still I can't seem to shake it, that kind of *desiccated* feeling, as if somehow my body is losing the clay it needs to keep holding itself together. And then there is the unexplained smell of bonfires, and the sea, and the pinpricks of rain . . . It all seems too unlikely to be quite feasible, and I am both concerned and embarrassed by it.

Perhaps a future version of myself could wake up one day feeling some incredible certainty about Beatrice, about London, and he'd seize the suitcase by the handle – no problem lifting it now, it'd be light as a feather – and then, wearing a crisp white shirt and newly polished shoes he'd stride down to this lake in Hyde Park – this very lake in front of us now – where he'd swing the suitcase high. And then, just as it was reaching the very pinnacle of its arc, he'd let it go, so that it soared out through the sky. It would hang in the air, then, suspended for one long moment, poised as the dominant forces acting on it switched from being the propulsive influences of his hurling it to simple gravity, tugging it down to the pond. In that moment, that moment of suspension, the covers of the book would flutter open, the notes of different currencies would fall out of their envelopes and mingle with each other, the keys would jangle, and the needle of the compass I put there this morning would stop all of its wild swinging and would finally correct itself, free at last of the confusing magnetic influence of the lost coins gathered in my coat lining. And I think – I feel instinctively – that in the very instant of the needle's settling on True North, the link between myself and the suitcase would be broken. Something closed and hidden deep in the centre of me would be released, and a fresh simplicity would enter my life. Then the suitcase would fall in the water, scattering ducks, and I'd watch it sink to the bottom, to the very heart of the lake.

Then, still dressed, of course, in sharp shirt and smart shoes, this other, clear-headed, parallel version of me would pull himself together and go and find a job, something useful, something normal – something in an office with floor-to-ceiling glass windows and a rubber plant, maybe – where he'd finally embrace the life he was so very lucky to have been granted, and at last slot into this blank space that has seemingly been allocated for him in the world, this space which seems to fit his personal dimensions quite exactly, though he can't recall ever asking for it to do so. He'll give up on all his questioning, all his rowing backwards, all his trying to fight against the tide. He'd go home to see his family three times a year and never complain that that's too little. In fact, it won't even occur to him, and he certainly won't still keep accidentally referring to it as *home*. He'll go to see his parents, take Beatrice with him, and everyone in Killorglin will be so glad to see them both. And though it will sadden him, of course, to see his dad get slowly worse, it won't draw defensive and scornful behaviour out of him, it won't lead to this complete and hopeless uncertainty about things, and it won't break him, as it is threatening to break him now. Because he will be capable, dependable: somebody who could go to a party, tell a stranger all about himself and keep his head held high, finally giving poor Beatrice something to be proud of.

I often think of how we met, back when we were both at college, at a party in one of those big houses in Dun Laoghaire. I didn't know the host – I'd been brought there by my brother, by Ciaran – I think I mentioned him before? – and it seems to me that Beatrice came across as being quite different in those days, as easygoing, almost. As someone quite relaxed, someone who could spill red wine over her dress and laugh. Her hair was longer, in any case, and she was studying for a degree in Anthropology, and I suppose her Englishness seemed quite exotic to me,

then. We fell to talking by the food table, and it being
something of a notioned affair – it was Dun Laoghaire,
after all – there was a full array of different snacks, with a
cheeseboard as the centrepiece. Before I knew what I was
doing, I was telling her all about Granda and the dairy,
about his goats and about his brother with the seaweed,
and then about how Nan and Granda always brought so
much cheese whenever they came across to visit that we ate
it at every meal for days, and how we'd always laugh at
Dad for smiling in that quiet way of his, obviously just so
proud to have this big family for his own parents to come
over to. And I don't know . . . I'm well aware it could
sound quite ridiculous, even absurd, as cheese is hardly
a romantic thing, at least not in conventional terms, but
sitting there with Beatrice I felt certain there was no one I
would rather share that with, in that moment – that goat's
cheese spread on soda bread, that close approximation of
the taste of home.

It's funny how much difference a few years can make.
Even months, even weeks, even two hundred and fourteen
days – or two hundred and fourteen and a half, if you're
counting today. Do you ever feel that when time passes,
it doesn't always take you with it? I often wonder if that's
how Dad must feel, now he's started to forget things. It's
particularly those things that happened to him recently,
and now it's like the weeks go past for everybody else, all

the rest of us moving faster and further away, while he's marooned, a still point.

But I should say, I think – I think it might be getting worse, the strange thing that keeps happening with my arm. I can feel it really quite strongly now, and it's also . . . moving around a little, I think, maybe in the muscles of my chest. It's . . . well, I'll be honest with you, it's got me worried. Like, honestly worried. What if I'm really sick? Or I've accidentally imbibed some kind of substance? And why is there never any sensible, accepted protocol for the things that actually do go wrong with you in life? Or for the things that seem to go wrong with me, anyway. Burns, fine; meningitis, concussion, heart attacks . . . I mean, I don't want to tempt fate but there's an accepted set of things a person can do in any of those circumstances, isn't there? A sequence of actions you can follow that will be the right ones, that will definitely, in all circumstances, be sensible and help you to get better. But what happens when you have no settled diagnosis? Don't you see? Until I know what's wrong with me I have no hope of finding a cure, or a treatment, or any kind of escape route from out of this trap of myself, from these tortured thoughts and sentences, from this condition and this pain inside my chest. You are following me, aren't you? You do understand what I mean?

*

Leanne takes a bite of her pizza and chews, staring at a duck skimming the surface of the Serpentine, landing on the water, tucking feathers and wings neatly underneath its body, ready to start swimming. Air, water, ducks. She lets Daniel's words float around the tops of both their heads, orbiting the bench for a while. Then she wipes her mouth on the sleeve of her jacket.

'Where's – what's her name? Beatrice? Where's Beatrice in all this?' she asks.

'I suppose she's at work right now,' Daniel says, and checks his watch. 'And then she'll be home around eight, or nine. She doesn't work far from our flat, but she works late. Sometimes she goes to the gym. She's very driven.'

'Do you love her enough?'

'What?'

'Simple question.' Leanne takes another bite of pizza, and rolls her head from side to side, stretching out her neck from where it has become stiff with her being slouched up against the bench while Daniel was talking. 'Do you love her?' she says.

'That's not what you asked the first time,' he says.

'I'm sorry?'

'The first time you said – do you love her *enough*.'

'It's more or less the same thing, though, isn't it?'

'I don't think so at all, no.'

'Well, do you have an answer?'

'To which question?'

'Oh, come on.'

'No, really, they are definitely not the same.'

'To "Do you love her enough?" then.'

'I – don't know. It's a very personal question. And – and it's rude to talk with your mouth full.'

Leanne sighs. 'You do want me to help, don't you?'

'I want somebody to help.'

'So . . .' Leanne stretches her neck out again.

'I mean, I want somebody to help, but obviously with caveats,' says Daniel. 'Not anyone with demonstrably bad judgement, or with obvious psychological problems.'

Leanne gives him a look. 'Well, what I would say – what I would say the weird thing is about this whole situation – is how little you talk about Beatrice.'

'I talk about Beatrice.'

'Not like a man engaged to be married to her.'

'No, I talk about her. I do. She's just . . . not quite the problem now. Or not the whole problem. She's not exactly what I'm worried about.'

'Why did you ask her to marry you?'

'I didn't.'

'You didn't?'

'No. I mean, she asked me. I couldn't ask her. I have no money, and no job.'

'Seriously?'

'Of course, seriously.'

'No, I mean, seriously that's why you didn't ask her? It's the twenty-first century, Daniel. Surely that kind of thing shouldn't matter any more.'

'Well then, she also had this position already lined up over here, and this whole plan for everything – all this furniture, enough saved for a deposit on a flat. And I just – I just couldn't—' Daniel breaks off, rubs his chest, his arm, massages the tendons of his wrist. 'Anyway, of course it matters. You're being wilfully naïve if you claim to think otherwise.'

Leanne raises an eyebrow. 'Jeez, you're a piece of work, aren't you?'

'What? No! I'm just – I'm just talking, or trying to.'

'So *she* asked *you* to marry her?'

'Yes, that's what I said.'

'And you said yes.'

'Obviously.'

'And why did you do that, Daniel?'

'Please stop interrogating me. I think it's making the weird thing with my arm worse.'

'I'm trying to help.'

'But you're not, you're not helping.'

'Daniel, you really are not my problem. I don't even know you.'

Daniel shifts round, then, on the bench to face her. 'Why are you looking at me like that?'

'I'm not looking at you like anything.'

'Yes, you are. You're pissed off. I can feel it.

'I'm not,' says Leanne. 'I'm not pissed off.'

'I'm sorry I pissed you off.'

'You didn't.'

'Yes, I did.'

'Don't argue with me. Only I know if you pissed me off.'

He doesn't reply to that, so for a while they sit in silence watching pigeons pecking around their shoes. Leanne checks her watch, and then throws her crumpled pizza wrappings over Daniel's head, neatly into the bin next to them.

'Look,' she says. 'I have to get back to work.'

'You work?'

'Of course I work. You think I just sit here all day, listening to weirdos on park benches?'

'Everybody in this city works.'

'Most people,' she says.

Some early daffodils are showing their shoots by the side of the path and Leanne stares at them as if they, somehow, might provide new insight into the conversation.

'Not you, though,' she says.

'No,' Daniel says.

Leanne keeps staring at the daffodils, checks her watch again, then yawns and rubs her eyes.

'Do you work nearby? Near to here?' asks Daniel.

'Yep. Just over there.' Leanne gestures to a building.

'But that's—'

'St Mary's Hospital.'

'That's not where you work.'

'Why not?'

'You don't seem anything like a doctor.'

'I'm a nurse.'

'And you definitely don't seem like a nurse.'

'How so? What do nurses seem like?'

'I don't know, I didn't mean – it's just . . . there's a certain harshness to your manner. It's not something I associate with nurses.'

'Excuse me?'

'You asked me. You asked me what I meant. And you must be aware of it, surely. After all, it's obviously a culti-vated thing. Or else it's natural and you've made no effort to disguise it, or to tone it down at all. But I can't seriously believe you're not self-aware enough to realise the way you come across. You don't seem stupid, after all.'

'Jesus Christ, I don't have time for this.' Leanne shuffles forward to get up off the bench. 'I only stopped to ask if you were feeling OK, you looked so wrecked. I don't need a character assassination.'

'No,' says Daniel. 'Wait, I'm sorry. I don't mean to be like this, I don't want to be like this. I just feel terrible, is all. Like something in me is breaking, or the whole of me is dissolving, and it's . . . difficult.'

Leanne sighs, seems to make some kind of decision, then turns back to face him. 'Where,' she says, 'where exactly is it painful?'

'What? Right now?'

'Yes, right now.'

'I don't know. Kind of . . . everywhere?'

'Nowhere more specific?'

'No. I don't know. I can't say.'

'Fine.' Leanne rolls her eyes, sinks her hands into her coat pockets and stands up. It's not quite spring enough yet to sit still outside for as long as she has done, and she's spent eight hours on her feet at work today already. Her bones hurt. She yawns and starts walking away, back into her afternoon. She considers leaving it at that with Daniel, but then says over her shoulder, 'I don't think it's a doctor you need. Figure out if you really love her. That's my advice.'

'Wait!' he says again, calling after her.

Leanne doesn't stop walking at first. And then she does.

'What?' she says, turning, hands in pockets. He'll make her late back to work, and what a fool she'd feel to get in trouble for something so avoidable as stopping to talk to someone like Daniel. Someone so self-absorbed, so basically objectionable – but then it's true there does seem something slightly . . . *off* about him. Something that sets her nurse's sixth sense tingling. Not that he's physically ill in the way he's obviously trying to hint at. She's seen men like him before: too clever for their own good and reaching out to her with vague, imagined symptoms, wanting sympathy, legitimacy, attention. But even so, there's definitely *something*.

And yet she's been gone far too long already. She shouldn't have left, really, with all the ward rounds to get done, and Maya, who'll be needing her hair washed, Douglas, who she should check on as soon as she gets back, and crash calls and beds to change and god knows whatever else that'll need doing. She shouldn't even have come out here at all. She stares at Daniel, weighs up that feeling of fundamental *wrongness*, and makes the calculation of whether staying for a moment will be worth it.

'Are you married?' he asks out of nowhere then, derailing her train of thought.

'Excuse me?'

'Please. I want to know.'

'Seriously?'

'Yes. Why not? Seriously.'

She checks her watch again: eight minutes, now, until she is expected back. She considers simply leaving. His expression, though, is too utterly sincere.

'Then no, Daniel. I am not married,' she tells him.

'Why not?' he says.

What a question for a stranger to ask.

And suddenly, just for a moment, everything feels as he described it – time moves forward, but it doesn't seem to take her with it. It doesn't take either of them.

A siren passes somewhere near them just outside the boundary of the park. A toddler stamps down in a crowd of pigeons. An ice-cream seller bursts into loud laughter at something someone says as they hand over the cash for a medium-sized cone of mint chocolate chip. Thousands of Londoners walk, stop, run, dance, kiss in the city around them – and Leanne thinks. First she thinks about saying something flippant, but then Daniel looks so goddamn desperate for some kind of answer that she really doesn't have the heart. So she lets her eyes drift back over to the patch of daffodil shoots again, and she lets herself remember. She remembers the guy who took her to Paris and then proposed on the train home. She remembers her college boyfriend, who used to turn up spontaneously at her apartment with flowers until he moved away for law school and everything fell apart. She remembers the guy who seemed so great on paper she stuck with him for two whole years even though they had nothing at all to say to each other. And she remembers her mother, making her a gift of her own grandmother's engagement ring on the morning of her twenty-first birthday. A sudden breeze makes her shiver, and a sparrow sings in Hyde Park.

'Why not?' Daniel still wants to know.

'Because,' she says, 'because honestly. Call me wilfully naïve about this, too, and who knows, I might be, I really, really might be – but honestly? I still believe –' Leanne looks up to the sky as if something about its expanse might serve to justify her words – 'I still think, that maybe some-day I'll meet someone. Someone who, well . . .' She closes her eyes, takes a breath, opens them again. 'Say I were an archaeological site,' she says.

'You're not an archaeological site,' says Daniel, frown-ing.

'Don't interrupt,' says Leanne. 'Say I was an archae-ological site, and people came and dug up my heart, and then they hinged it open, to find out what was in there. All they would find inside would be him. Only him, inside my heart. That's the person I'm waiting to meet. If that makes any sense at all.'

'I don't think that's wilfully naïve.'

'Yeah. Well. Maybe not.'

'I don't know what would be inside my heart,' Daniel says, then, 'if they dug it up – the archaeologists. I don't even know if they'd be able to find it. The heart archaeologists.'

Then for the first time this afternoon the clouds lift a little from his expression, and his face lights up with a dopey half-smile, probably at the idea of heart archaeologists. Leanne finds she's smiling back at him, though for a different reason entirely.

'It's just,' he says, 'it's like something in me is missing, or defective – not necessarily my heart, but still something important, something that should be at the very centre of me, but isn't. And the result is that I'm neither one thing nor the other, neither here nor there.'

All the frenetic, nervous energy seems to drain out of him as he says that. She notices he's looking at her properly now, too, for the first time since they started talking. And she finds, for some reason, that she doesn't quite know what to say.

'You'll be all right,' she tells him eventually, though that feels too pat, too banal, too certain. 'I wasn't from round here either, originally. The first year is hard. But you get used to it.'

'I hope so,' he says.

She tries her best to give him a reassuring nod, and

then, despite the part of herself still telling her not to leave him on his own, she turns and continues on, down the path.

She doesn't look back until she's most of the way around the lake, when she stops and scans the line of benches across the water, trying to pick Daniel out through the crowds of ambling, jogging, power-walking, strolling afternoon people thronging the path. And there he is, surely – that dark figure in the distance. He's rummaging around in his coat pockets, now, apparently looking for something, searching more frantically with every second that passes – patting his pockets from the outside, shaking the fabric out, gathering it up in his fists and squeezing it, as if feeling for something hidden in the lining . . . and then a group of mothers pushing babies in giant buggies blocks her view of him for a moment. She waits for them to pass, rubbing her tired, tired eyes, and then she sees something that just can't be right. She's too far away, that must be it. There's too much glare in the afternoon light to make things out properly, or she's got the wrong bench, or both. Because it seems simply too unlikely, not least because it's March, and there are green shoots starting to show on the branches above her.

But there it is, all the same: a cloud of autumn leaves: gold and brown; russet and honey and burnt sugar and holly-berry red; and they're swirling and curling their ways up around the bench and towards the clouds in a shape that seems to have nothing to do with the swift, light breezes of the early spring day. It reminds Leanne first of a hurricane, then of a dust storm, then of a double helix.

And then the March wind blows strong and cold on the back of her neck and the pattern is violently disrupted, the spiral broken and the leaves dispersed; the golds and the reds and the burning ambers scattered, and thrown high up into this open window of sky, this blank space at London's core, framed on all sides by tower blocks and high-rises but so clear here, above the park.

Then the leaves have risen higher than the buildings, dancing on air currents blowing hot and cold – currents that Leanne is far too low down to feel, still on the ground as she is. Each leaf seems to her now like a tiny, bright feather, shed from the wings of some autumnal, fiery bird.

But there's still a figure sitting there, left behind on the bench. Maybe Daniel had the leaves in his pockets. Maybe he'd been waiting for her to go before he threw handfuls of them out and up in the air. Though he hadn't seemed all that erratic, in the end – only a little anxious, and a little sad. And then, is that even him that she can see, over there, on the bench, on the other side of the lake? There are just too many people rushing up and down the path in front of it for her to be certain. And the light is too bright and too dazzling on the water. From here the figure looks less like an actual person than a rough pencil sketch of a man. Or even like a coat, shirt, trousers and shoes laid out to dry in the sun by someone with a sense of humour. Maybe she'll see Daniel again, sometime. Maybe then she'll ask about the leaves.

What was with all the leaves? she'll say.

Oh, the leaves, he'll say. *Funny you should ask about the leaves, because* – and then he'll talk on about the suitcase again, or the compass, or the coins – or about his grandparents back on that island, and the way that goat's cheese flecked with seaweed always makes him think of home.

Shearing Season

Once upon a time, there lived a strangely gifted eleven-year-old called Jamie. He liked trains, and planes, and spaceships, and he wanted to be an astronaut. He lived, however, in the middle of the Lake District, on a remote sheep farm. No one in his family or his small community knew the first thing about how to break into the space travel industry, or indeed even the first thing about outer space.

Jamie's mum, though, had a computer. It was just a wheezy old desktop with a terrible internet connection that lived in the corner of her bedroom, but Jamie would spend hours every day sitting glued to the monitor, waiting patiently through long minutes of buffering as he watched his favourite YouTube videos. The best ones were grainy NASA footage from the sixties and seventies: successful rocket launches, failed rocket launches, satellites falling into the Earth's orbit . . . and then there was the moon landing, of course. He watched that one over and over until he could act it out with his eyes shut, doing all the different noises and voices that cropped up on the audio track.

'*Crrssk Crrssk* – Roger, Houston. Loud and clear! – *Crrssk Crrsk,*' he would practise saying to himself in his best American twang.

Jamie's mum often had lodgers staying at the farm. They would usually arrive in the spring, just after the lambing, around the time the first swallows appeared. Jamie never paid much attention to these itinerant members of the household as he was always too busy with schoolwork or chores or with YouTube – too busy, that is, until a tangle-haired, scrawny young man named Miles arrived at the farm one afternoon in shearing season, complete with references and some official-looking papers declaring him to be a PhD student in Aerospace Engineering. Jamie didn't know what this meant, exactly, but he knew an opportunity when he saw one. He introduced himself to Miles one morning while Miles, always quite a late riser, was still spreading marmalade on his toast.

As Miles stared, chewing steadily, Jamie explained to him that he was going to be an astronaut just as soon as he'd decided on what the best route for him would be – whether he'd prefer to approach NASA first, or the European Space Agency, and then whether he'd like to train to be a pilot astronaut or decide to develop areas of expertise elsewhere. Jamie had done his research and spoke airily, but the truth of it was that his heart was pounding. If only this new lodger would recognise him as a kindred spirit, as someone with the capacity to learn. Miles' expression, though, remained one of almost dizzying blankness and Jamie didn't know what to think. At last, though, Miles finished his last bite of toast, pushed his thick-rimmed glasses up his nose, and began to speak in what Jamie felt certain was a faintly Californian accent.

'Sure,' Miles said. 'That makes sense. NASA definitely has the better funding opportunities, but I do see how the European Space Agency could be the more interesting of the two, from an international relations point of view, at least.'

Jamie blinked. He had never heard a real-life person speak in such a way.

'And then of course the European Space Agency does also have the advantage of being relatively local.'

He spoke as if these places were completely real. Which they were – Jamie knew that, of course – but it was as if they were almost commonplace to Miles, part of his everyday vocabulary and concerns.

'Why did you come here?' Jamie couldn't help asking him then. 'When you could have been working with real scientists, real astronauts, somewhere in a desert or a city, or even in Hawaii?'

'I came looking for peace,' was all Miles said. And he brushed the crumbs off his fingertips, pushed his chair back from the table, and went to wash his plate up at the sink. 'How far have you got with your studies?' he asked as he rinsed off the soap suds. 'Maybe I could help, if you'd like.'

First, Miles said, just to get started, Jamie should get his sketchpad, go into another room, and draw a picture of what he thought 'effervescent' looked like. Jamie wasn't quite sure why this was relevant but of course he didn't question it. He rushed off to the living room where he sharpened his best pencils, laid all his coloured pens and crayons out in rows across the coffee table, and unwrapped his new Saturn-shaped eraser from its packaging. Working there, tongue sticking out, deep in concentration, he drew on his sketchpad a curious vortex of stars and smiles and comets all zooming about the place, mixed in with a few cheerful-looking sheep, limbs akimbo in starry space. It took him all morning and into the afternoon, and he even forgot about lunch as he tried his best to capture the specific sort of dynamism he associated with 'effervescent'.

When he was finished, he showed it to Miles.

Miles just nodded. 'Yes, I see,' he said. 'But you haven't even tried to get in the grittier aspects of "effervescent" – the grainy, gravelly shades of it that catch the light so deeply when the sun hangs at a certain angle. Or the flatter, oily patches that you can often find just next to those gravelly parts – the patches that reflect that sunlight back as rainbow stains. What about those? Were they just too

hard to draw in the end? I appreciate it's difficult to capture them, seeing as it's all about reflection of light. Still, if
you'd like to understand space you'll certainly need to be
comfortable working with light. You may not think so now
but it's a crucial aspect of the job.'

Jamie was disappointed. He'd tried hard, and was sure
he'd done his best. That was what Mrs Walker at school
always said, after all. *You just do your best, poppet, and
that'll be grand.* Still, looking at Miles as he sat there
now – cross-legged on the floor in a storm of wonderfully
incomprehensible-seeming papers – Jamie knew, somehow,
that he had moved into a completely different realm from
anything that could be learnt in Mrs Walker's class. He
swallowed his urge to cry about the picture, and kept his
mouth shut.

'Think about it,' Miles told him, 'and when you've
considered it properly draw me a picture of "perspective".
Not a picture *using* perspective, that is, but a picture *of*
perspective itself.'

Determined to do everything exactly right this time,
Jamie left behind his pencils and his sketchpad, and went
straight to his room to sit and think hard about how
he could have missed the grittier, reflective aspects of
'effervescent'. And by the time his mum called up finally
announcing dinner was ready he did think that maybe he'd

cracked what Miles had meant, or at least that he'd spent a respectable amount of time trying to, anyway.

Dinner that day was his favourite: smiley potato faces, fishfingers and peas. Except that he couldn't concentrate properly on enjoying it at all, he was so caught up in thinking about all the strange things that had happened while his mum had been out on the farm with the sheep. He couldn't concentrate on anything she was saying, either, as she sat opposite him worrying aloud about how each of the new lambs was faring, and about how long it always took to get through a whole farm's worth of shearing, and then also whether Jamie thought Miles might be appearing soon. Because she didn't like to shout up again but if he didn't hurry his fishfingers would be cold. And was Miles definitely eating properly? Only it seemed like he was always missing mealtimes, and she couldn't help but fret a little. And come to think of it, talking of Miles, it was lovely to see them getting on so well, but would Jamie be able to spare a moment to come out to the farm tomorrow, to help with all the shearing?

Jamie couldn't wait to get away and start on 'perspective'. He bolted his food and left most of his peas unfinished, grabbing his sketchpad and pencils and dashing back upstairs as fast as he could, to the quiet of his room. He slammed the door and took a moment to recover his breath. Then he selected his sharpest, most impressive-looking pencil and set out a blank sheet of paper. This time, he tried to think hard about his subject in all of its nuances – the light and the dark and the gritty and the smooth – and in the end he had to use two whole sheets of his A3 sketchbook, torn out and taped together on the reverse side. It was the only way he could get a big enough canvas – the concept simply needed so much space.

The picture turned out considerably sparser than the one he had drawn for 'effervescent'. 'Perspective' was a lone piece of space junk floating out into a void of zero gravity, with the small figure of an astronaut sitting on top of it, helmet angled so it was clear he was looking back towards Earth – which appeared as a little watery sphere in the very far right-hand corner. Jamie had been careful this time not to overpopulate the space between the two focus points with sparkles and comets. He'd really thought about the cold emptiness between stars, and had focused everything on capturing that chilly void, shading all the subtlety he could into this absence of light with every grade of pencil he had at his disposal.

Eventually, at about 5 a.m., he decided that he'd done the best he could, and collapsed into bed to get a few hours' rest.

*

He woke late, around nine, but when he rushed down to the kitchen in a panic Miles was only just pouring out what looked to be his first cup of coffee of the morning.

'I've done it!' Jamie said, as Miles blinked at him, owl-like through his glasses. 'I've cracked "perspective"!'

Miles seemed instantly to wake up at this, and, leaving his coffee behind, they strode off together to see the finished piece.

When they got there, though, Miles simply stood in front of it with a frown etched between his chaotic eyebrows. Then, still without a word, not even a hint as to roughly what his verdict might be, he squinted his eyes and began to tip his head from side to side, as if trying the picture out from different angles. It was almost too much for Jamie. After all those hours of concentration and so little sleep he wanted only a hug and a pat on the back, or else to stamp and to shout at Miles all in a rush, *Just tell me now, do I have what it takes to be an astronaut or not?* Still, something told him it was important to let Miles finish, and so somehow he managed to contain himself, and wait. Miles finished tipping his head, and made a series of grave-sounding *hmm*-ing noises, which really could have meant anything.

'There's too much story here,' he said, at last. 'You've got the basic idea, yes, but there's too much of a narrative. You don't need it and it's covering all the perspective up with something else – a story about an astronaut being far away from home. I didn't ask for that story, it was the *perspective* I was after.'

Jamie was crestfallen. Tired and overworked, he stormed off to the bathroom, locking himself in for a tantrum and a good cry.

After a while he felt better, washed his face, and went to the kitchen for some water. Miles was waiting for him with a pot of mint tea, freshly brewed.

'I'm sorry if I upset you with my reaction to your "perspective",' Miles said, handing Jamie a teacup and saucer without any apparent doubt that he would take it. 'I sometimes misjudge how I appear to other people. Your work so far has been exceptional. I only criticise where I aim to improve.'

Jamie accepted the mint tea without complaint, though he would never usually drink so adult a beverage. He blew on its murky surface and wondered if this was another kind of lesson.

'There's just one more thing I need you to try,' Miles said, sipping the boiling liquid without even wincing. 'Then we'll know whether you've got what it takes to comprehend space or not.'

Jamie, buoyed up by Miles' admission that his work had been 'exceptional', asked what this last thing was.

'I'd like you to draw me "The Unknown",' said Miles.

'"The Unknown"?' asked Jamie.

'"The Unknown",' affirmed Miles.

'But how can I—' began Jamie.

'Nope.' Miles cut him off mid-speech, raising a hand with absolute authority. 'I can't tell you. Just think about it. Think about what you've learnt.'

This couldn't be his final challenge. It was impossible, surely. It didn't make sense. But the conversation was over, that much was clear. It was time for Jamie to leave and he did so, noticing the unfairness of this only when he was halfway through the door. Because why should he be dismissed from his own kitchen?

And yet, *Then we'll know whether you've got what it takes to comprehend space or not*, Miles had said, hadn't he? And despite everything, Jamie still wanted to know the answer to that, more than anything. What would happen if it turned out that he did have what it took? Maybe Miles would introduce Jamie to all his Aerospace Engineering friends, and then as a surprise for his birthday they'd all get together and enrol him on a secret NASA fast-track training programme for young astronauts where he'd meet lots of other children from places like New York and Hong Kong and Tokyo, places where they'd never even heard of sheep farming at all, and they would all become great friends and train and go on missions together and even land on the moon. And then aside from all that – separate from his hopes and his dreams and ambitions – Miles simply wasn't like anyone Jamie had ever met before, and he didn't want to let him down. Because Miles had . . . what was the word? *Gravitas*. That was it. If Jamie had been drawing a picture of 'gravitas', he'd have drawn Miles.

But he wasn't drawing 'gravitas'. He was drawing 'The Unknown', and who knew how to start going about that? He thought until the sun was high over the hills and shining hot through the glass of his window. Then the clock chimed twelve in the kitchen below, and all in a rush Jamie knew what he would do. He set himself up in the linen cupboard with a blank sheet of paper on an easel and a box of sharpened pencils, and then he checked carefully that everything was in position and that he knew exactly where everything was, before shutting himself in the dark.

Jamie worked blind in that cupboard for five whole hours. Initially he worried that his eyes would adjust, but the darkness was absolute, muffled into a soft, stuffy texture by the sheets folded up all around him.

As he sketched, he sustained a particular kind of balancing act, holding in his mind simultaneously all the contradictory, paradoxical elements of 'The Unknown'. How liberating a concept it could be, for instance, in that it was impossible to plan for incorrectly, and how much hope it could bring in being able to encompass even the things everyone says are impossible. And then, of course, there was how much 'The Unknown' worried his mother. How she listened to the weather forecast several times throughout the day with that particular look on her face every time, just before the radio man spoke and explained what would happen – that was a side to 'The Unknown', too. Also, there was how Jamie himself felt in the moments before Miles told him what to draw next or what he thought about one of his pictures – and then there were Miles' curiously empty eyes – and, now Jamie came to consider it, how different 'The Unknown' was from the way his life had always been up till now; how 'The Unknown' could maybe even provide something of an escape route from the repetitive rhythms from season to season of a life lived in a world surrounded on all sides by sheep.

Jamie was, though, careful not to let any one consideration dominate. Instead he tried his best to hold his mind in a state of pure possibility and uncertainty, his reasoning here being based on the immense fragility of 'The Unknown', in that the very second it becomes substantial enough to think about in concrete terms, it stops being itself. The one constant he allowed himself was the memory of the sensation of seeing something only in the corner of his eye. He channelled this principle through the whole process – never once contemplating the subject of his work directly, and keeping 'The Unknown' in the corner of his mind.

When he felt as if the work might be complete, he opened the cupboard door to let in the light, blinked a few times at the canvas, and was content with what he saw.

He went looking for Miles.

Miles was at his desk in his room, building a structure out of odd assorted objects – a packet of staples, a few lengths of string, what looked roughly like a quarter of a pack of cards, a half-burnt-out tealight . . . Jamie watched him for a while from the landing before knocking on the open door.

'What is it?' asked Miles, without looking up from his project.

'I've finished it,' Jamie told him.

Miles was trying to balance a pencil vertically on the edge of a protruding ruler. He failed, and the whole construction collapsed. He removed his glasses, rubbed his eyes, replaced his glasses, then finally he looked at Jamie.

'That's not possible,' he said.

'Well, I've done it anyway,' Jamie told him.

Jamie led the way to 'The Unknown'.

From the little that he knew of him, Jamie sensed Miles wasn't the sort of person ever to appear perturbed or excited but, Jamie realised as they walked, this was definitely the first time Miles had taken his lead and followed him anywhere. Jamie had always been the one following Miles.

When they reached the linen cupboard Jamie opened the door and held it for Miles like an old-fashioned servant. Miles stepped inside, and Jamie watched from the corridor as he took in the drawing.

'"The Unknown",' he breathed.

'I told you,' Jamie said, but Miles wasn't listening.

Staring instead at the phenomenon on the easel before him, Miles exhaled in what sounded to Jamie like a sigh of profound relief. A slow, hazy smile spread out over his features, and then he began to advance towards the picture, reaching out his arms as if to bask in it, or embrace it.

'It's beautiful,' he said, simply, before he stepped clean off this planet and straight into the fabric of Jamie's picture itself.

It was all very neatly done. There was hardly any fuss, only a momentary sense of visual disorder in the air around the easel, and a sound that put Jamie in mind of bright shards of mineral-rich rock pouring down over black sandpaper. To witness it you'd have thought people stepped out of linen closets and into pencil drawings every day.

A few moments after Miles had gone, Jamie went to examine his picture. It was almost completely unchanged, except, when he looked very carefully, he was sure he could see a few Miles-like features flashing in fragments through its vortex of visual ideas – just a few strands of untidy hair here, the corner of a glasses frame there, a shoelace, the bright flash of a tooth. Jamie passed his eyes over each of these in turn, and experienced a feeling of moral uncertainty.

'Thank you,' he thought he heard the fragments breathe.

After a while, he shut the door to the linen cupboard, and went to find his mother in the shearing shed. He helped her with the sheep for the rest of the afternoon, and then when it was dark they both went into the kitchen and made hot chocolate together, properly, by melting real pieces of chocolate into molten goodness and stirring it into the milk.

Jamie's mum asked whether Miles was about, and whether she needed to cook dinner, and Jamie worried then – as he'd been trying not to worry all afternoon – that she'd find out about what had happened, whatever it was he had done. So he smiled widely as if there were nothing amiss and told her that she needn't cook tonight because Miles had left already, and had gone off into 'The Unknown'. Part of him did wonder what he would say if she asked him what he meant by 'The Unknown', or even asked him what he thought about it. The idea, though, simply didn't seem to occur to Jamie's mum, who only sighed, rubbed her eyes, and said that she was hungry anyway. So they stood at the stove and made pancakes with lemon and sugar, and she turned on the radio for the weather forecast and it played in the background as they ate, filling the room with talk of low pressure and oncoming rain. And then, later on in the evening, Jamie read her stories from the paper as she did some mending by the fire. By that point Jamie felt so comforted and humbled by the familiarity of it all that it was almost as if Miles had never come to the farm at all.

By ten o'clock, though, Jamie's mum had gone to bed, and Jamie wasn't tired. He sat up feeding bits of wood into the fire until he couldn't stand it any longer, and went back to the linen closet to look at his impossible drawing. Seeing it again like that, in the light of the lamp on the landing, he knew there could be no doubt at all about what had happened that afternoon.

He stepped into the closet himself, and stared at the picture. And he wondered, then, what would happen if he opened his mind just a little wider, stretched out his arms, and advanced towards it – just as Miles had done.

He wondered, but he didn't try it. He tore his eyes away before he changed his mind, closed the cupboard door, and went into the kitchen to put some oats on to soak for his mum's breakfast, before taking himself smartly off to bed. He didn't worry too much more about 'The Unknown' that night. He knew where it was, if he wanted it.

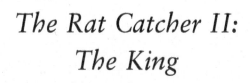

The Rat Catcher II:
The King

I'd been asked for by the king himself, or so that scrawny messenger boy had said, when he'd knocked on my door all those days ago. So how, then, had it come to pass that I found myself regaining consciousness in the woods with the strong suspicion I'd been poisoned by my own powder? I understood very little as I lay there in the snow, my skin freezing and my bones aching and my stomach cramping and my head thumping something terrible. I only knew I didn't want to think about Ethel – about how she'd invited me to walk with her in the deserted parks and been the only one present when I'd swallowed the wine. How she'd brought the wine, even, and poured out for me. I didn't want to think of her and so I set my sights on that tell-tale curl of smoke instead, standing out from the trees against the fading light of yet another frozen evening. I'd been poisoned while undertaking royal orders, after all, so perhaps the king was the one I should look to for an explanation, and Ethel hadn't been at fault at all.

My progress through the woods was excruciating. I was always stumbling on roots, or leaning on trees to cough or catch my breath, and on one occasion I even had to stop completely while I doubled over into a most undignified position, vomiting what I hoped was the last of the Emerald Dust from my system. I found I had to whistle tunes at random just to give myself the strength to keep my feet stepping forward. I was loud, then, in my movements, and it wasn't only rats I sensed moving out of my path, although they were surely amongst the parade of forest creatures I heard scurrying away ahead of me, their little feet disturbing twigs and snow and layers of dead leaves. They would be those staggeringly fat palace rats, no doubt, with their sleek coats and curving fangs and twisting, wormlike tails. I pictured them clambering and sliding over each other in their hurry to get away, the mass of them gathering in strength until they were like a tide of wriggling rodent bodies, a river of which I was the source. Out of all the creatures in the forest, only the crows seemed glad to see me, circling above in the dim evening sky. You couldn't blame them. I must have seemed a dead man walking, with my juddering stoop and unseemly, mincing tread, the best I could manage after being so transfigured by the poison, and by the hours spent out in the cold. Still, I maintained my focus on the task at hand and tracked my way towards the smoke until eventually I lost sight of it completely. Which meant, of course, it must be close.

I raised my nose into the air and sniffed. *There*. Woodsmoke, on the breeze. I followed the hot, musty scent of it until I came upon a clearing, and a cabin in the woods. I say cabin: it was a wooden structure in the style of a cabin but really, in most neighbourhoods of the city, a place that size would have passed for a mansion. It even had a chimney, which was where the smoke was coming from. That made me pause a moment. I'd been expecting something altogether more rudimentary. A bonfire, perhaps. A jolly and informal picture of life in the great outdoors.

I limped up to the door and the high barking of some small dog started up inside. I never have liked dogs, especially small ones, but I didn't hesitate or change my mind. I raised my fist to knock . . . but then the door was swinging open before my knuckles could quite reach it, the blessed warmth of the fire was wafting its way out towards me, and suddenly there was a mangy creature snapping and barking round my ankles, and a boy standing there. Or – I do apologise – a *young gentleman* would probably be more accurate. Only, he'd let his hair grow long, his face was covered all in dirt, and from the smell of him he hadn't washed in weeks so I didn't recognise him, quite, at first. It was him all right, though. The young king. Although looking a lot less regal now than he'd done at the coronation. Quite a different man without all the pomp and circumstance.

I had, I think, been planning on saying something like this –

It is quite the honour to meet you, Your Majesty. I myself, if you were wondering, am the rat catcher that you sent for directly following your coronation. I present myself to you this evening to make some respectful enquiries concerning the nature of my employment. Chief among them, how it came to pass that I was gravely poisoned in the process of undertaking my duties in your palace – almost killed, that is to say. But also to enquire whether indeed you might have some advice or even help that you could offer me in this predicament of mine . . .

But there was something about the sight of him there: a skinny boy out in the woods, all alone with only this scrap of a dog for company. I looked him up and down.

'I see,' I said instead, hardly knowing I was speaking the words out loud. 'If you take the fancy clothes away, and all the servants, and all the fuss, even a king looks just like anybody else.'

He narrowed his eyes while the dog kept yapping. It was all I could do not to kick it. Then he laughed – a high, loud kind of laugh that jangled in my ears.

'How very amusing,' he said. 'I'd been hoping for a visitor. The long evenings out here are –' he padded away from me as he spoke, back into the cabin, and I saw his shirt was torn and he wasn't wearing shoes – 'they are so very dull, you see. Well, don't just stand there. Come in. Entertain me.'

I stepped over the dog and over the threshold, the second royal residence I'd been invited into within the space of a week, I couldn't help but notice.

There was no furniture. Not even curtains. Only the fire burning in a rudimentary hearth at one end of the room and a nest of blankets in the opposite corner, where I had to assume both he and the dog slept, for there was no other basket or blanket anywhere else in the place that might have done for the creature. Revolting, I always think, this business of animals and humans living close together like that. It doesn't seem natural to me. I scanned the room for evidence of rats. Strangely, though – very strangely, given the ferocity of the infestation in both the city and the palace – there were hardly any signs at all. Only a single hole in the base of the far wall of a size to suggest nothing more than perhaps one or two small mice.

I should have spoken my concerns as soon as I'd stepped inside. I should have dared to demand an explanation and have been done with it. Yet it was quite as if my voice had been stolen from me, snatched clean out of my mouth by the unexpected nature of the scene. Back in the woods I'd imagined, I think, that the king might ask me for the reason why I'd come – from his seat upon a rustic throne, perhaps – thus granting me permission to launch into my complaint. As it was, I only felt uncomfortable. I couldn't think where to begin.

There was an unfinished jigsaw puzzle on the floor not far from the hearth and, in search of a distraction, I made my way over there. The picture it showed was of a country scene: blue sky, green hills, a skein of birds in mid-flight, trees with all their leaves on them, and a river flowing through the whole of it, until it was stopped by the running out of jigsaw pieces. Or by the king's lack of progress, that is, in the matter of completing his puzzle.

'Very pretty, Your Majesty,' I told him.

The king was playing with his dog, dangling something in the air above its snout, then whipping it away again just before the mangy creature leapt up for it. It seemed a cruel sort of game to me, though I couldn't tell at all what the dog itself felt about it, if anything. It was one of those animals with sagging, squashed-up features – the ones that always seem dissatisfied whatever they are faced with.

I returned to studying the jigsaw puzzle.

'Couldn't be more different, really, from the way things are here,' I said, after a while.

The king turned to me, leaving his dog to snatch whatever it was from out of his slack fingers. He wandered over to stare at the puzzle from the other side.

'An interesting observation, Mr Rat Catcher. At least – you *are* the rat catcher, aren't you? Though why you are here is a mystery, when you were *meant* to be at the palace, making havoc for my sister. Oh, but in any case, how right you are, Mr Rat Catcher. It *is*, absolutely, the exact opposite of the environment in which we find ourselves. Although, would you not agree, there is something so very amusing about this particular little cabin, in so far as that question of *location* is concerned? You see, shut up inside like this with just dear Lucas here for company, I feel as if it could be almost anywhere – anywhere at all! – and that I could simply step out of my front door to find not the frozen forest there but, perhaps, this scene from my puzzle . . . Oh, and then how little Luke and I would scream for joy. We'd skip across the grassy plains and clamber up the trees like peasant boys in pastoral diversions, would we not, Lucas, dear?'

He turned away and stooped to scoop the dog into his arms, tucking its furry head right into the space under his chin so that I was faced with the sight of the two of them together, one set of features on top of the other.

'Oh, we would, wouldn't we?' the king continued. 'We'd lark about like anything, and then when the sun was quite high and we were both too hot to carry on – oh, but imagine, indeed, being too hot! Except I cannot really imagine it, having been frozen in this way for so very long . . . never mind, though, little Luke, we push on! So, being far too hot to carry on larking and sporting in the manner in which we had been previously, we would both dash down this way, *here* –' he crouched down next to the puzzle and traced his finger over it as if it were a map, still holding 'little Luke', as he called him, under one arm – 'through the fields, down the hills . . . to the river! Where you would swim, little Luke. Indeed, so would we both, I imagine, for I could not trust you to stay afloat alone in such a strong current, now, could I? No, you would be quite washed away from me, I dare say you would—'

The king broke off to nuzzle the creature into his face. It only sniffed at him, as if wishing he were a piece of food. Come to think of it, both the king and his small dog were looking little more than skin and bone. What was it, I wondered, that they ate out here?

'But there is no river outside,' said the king, as he sat down on the floor. 'And I can feel from here that it is as cold as it always is. But never mind, little Luke, never mind.'

I stared down at the king as he fiddled with a jigsaw piece, a bit of sky, playing at feeding it to Luke.

'Do you tell jokes, Mr Rat Catcher?' he asked me, without looking up. 'Or sing songs? Do you dance?'

'No, Your Majesty,' I said.

'And why do you look so very ugly? I was quite frightened, watching you limp up to my front door like that. You do seem quite the ghoul. Although in that, at least, you have my sympathies.' He dropped his voice to a whisper and put on a pantomime mimicry of my own accent – '*I've never been much of a looker myself,*' he said – and then he laughed that awful, jangling, high-pitched laugh of his again. 'Oh, but how marvellous, little Luke. It seems we have a new character!' And here he put on his pageantry version of my voice again. '*Mr Rat Catcher,*' he said, and quite dissolved in laughter.

'I'd appreciate it if you did not mock me, Your Majesty,' I said.

'*I'd appreciate it if you did not mock me, Your Majesty,*' he repeated back at me.

I didn't reply, but I did take a single step forward, treading on a section of his puzzle, breaking the connected pieces apart under my shoe. The idiot smile left his face, only to be replaced with big, innocent eyes I trusted even less.

'Oh, but I was only having fun, Mr Rat Catcher. We are so dull out here, you see, little Luke and I. And what else can we do to entertain ourselves if you will not sing for us or dance or tell us jokes? Can you do *anything*, Mr Rat Catcher? Or is there no hope for us at all?'

'I can catch rats.'

'Well, evidently. And goodness knows how useful that can be.' The king frowned and paused a moment, as if waiting for some unpleasant thought to leave him before continuing. 'But it is hardly something amusing, now, is it?'

'It could be,' I said. 'People have admired my traps. They've even been called . . .' But here I had to break off for a moment. I was still weak from my trek through the woods, and besides, there was something caught in my throat. I coughed and started my sentence again. 'They've even been called beautiful,' I said.

The king doubled over in laughter, poking at the dog, which was now squirming in his lap and looking, so far as I could tell, as if it were trying to get away from its master's rough handling.

'*They've even been called beautiful,*' said the king, in his version of my voice. 'Oh, but I do *like* this one, little Luke. He's the best character we've had in ages.' Then he made some effort to compose himself, looking up at me with a face full of exaggerated curiosity. 'But who, indeed, if I may enquire of you, my dear Mr Rat Catcher, has bestowed such an accolade upon your traps? Do tell, or else little Luke and I shall not believe you.'

'Miss Ethel,' I said. 'Miss Ethel at the palace told me my trap was beautiful, and you can disbelieve it all you like but it's true. The absolute and honest truth.'

'My sister?' said the king, and he stood up quite suddenly, dropping the dog to the floor as if he'd quite forgotten the mite was a living thing at all – although Luke looked accustomed to landing on his feet, that much was clear enough. He scuttled off to the blankets in the corner, probably grateful to no longer be the focus of his master's attention.

'Really?' said the king. 'Are you quite sure? How very strange. Though, of course, she must have had her reasons. Oh, but do tell me,' he advanced towards me, breaking his own jigsaw puzzle with the tread of his bare feet, 'what did you make of my sister, Mr Rat Catcher?'

'She seemed,' I began, and the ever-present question of the poison danced once again on the tip of my tongue. 'She seems a very charming young woman,' I said.

'*A very charming young woman*,' said the king. 'Oh, how gentlemanly of you – such old-fashioned courtesy. You are right, Mr Rat Catcher. She really is most charming, my sister. Or so it seems until you look a little closer. Did you meet Shaw up there, by any chance, Mr Rat Catcher? You can recognise him by his sycophancy – or his syco-phancy to my sister, at least, I should say. He would like nothing better than to give her the crown. Which is why he spends his days in scouring my poor dear father's will for any clause or even comma that he might construe as sufficient means to drive me further out than, indeed, I've hidden myself away already. I'm sure I cannot see why anyone should be so very fond of her. Can you think of why? Even my mother didn't like her, and my mother, Mr Rat Catcher, is widely held to have been something of an angel. Oh, but there's matter untoward going on between them, no doubt – between my sister and Shaw. I cannot help but suspect it. Well, did you see him?'

· 'I did, Your Majesty.'

'And what was he up to, tell me? Laughing? Dancing? Manufacturing a myriad of legal reasons why I must stay out here in this little home of mine and not come near that rat-infested seat of power they both so love to dwell in? Except – how silly of me – Shaw never laughs or dances. He doesn't even smile, as far as I'm aware. Do tell, Mr Rat Catcher, I want to know. My sister really called your traps *beautiful*, did she?'

'One of them, Your Majesty,' I said. 'I showed her only one of my traps, but yes. She called it beautiful. She did.'

'How curious of her. Oh but, Mr Rat Catcher, you do realise now that you shall have to show me, too? It would not be fair to show one of us and not the other.'

'I'm afraid that's impossible, Your Majesty.'

'But how on earth can it be *impossible*?' he said. 'You showed her well enough, why can you not show me?'

'I only meant, Your Majesty, that the trap in question is currently in use. And in any case, I would rather not revisit that particular one, is all.'

'Oh,' he said, and flashed a grin. 'How intriguing. Could it be that it brings up certain *painful memories*, Mr Rat Catcher? Concerning the most charming wiles of your *Miss Ethel*?'

'Not at all, Your Majesty,' I told him.

'Poor Mr Rat Catcher,' he said. 'My sister can be so reckless with other people's hearts. It's not her fault, you understand. That's simply what happens when you raise a child without love.'

And then he yawned, as though he'd uttered nothing more than some simple pleasantry about the weather, before shambling off back to his pile of blankets, scooping Luke out from the tangled mess of them.

'You must make us a new trap, Mr Rat Catcher,' he said, when Luke was clamped within his arms again. 'In fact, I do command it. And if we like it, I might even be persuaded to give you some advice as a reward. Mightn't I, little Luke? Yes, indeed – it's true! I might be induced to tell this nasty, ugly man just how he might patch things up with his favourite *Miss Ethel*, yes.'

'You could tell me something more about Miss Ethel?'

'Why, of course! I do reward good citizens, you know. I am not quite such a tyrant as all that. You do want to become friends with my sister, don't you?'

'Is it not what any man would want?' I said. And the nagging hope flickered in my brain again that there might be some other explanation for what had happened by the lake – that the lawyer, or the crone, or even the king might be behind my poisoning. But perhaps I should not have replied quite as I did, for something about what I said seemed to make the king's expression darken.

'How lucky I am,' he said, 'to have quite so *fascinating* a sibling.' And he kicked the remainder of his jigsaw puzzle, scattering the pieces all around the floor. 'It was ruined already. The only thing for it was to start again.'

He returned to his nest of blankets and sat down, letting go his hold of little Luke, who circled round his master for a moment, only, for some reason, to climb right back up into his lap of his own accord. As the king ran his hands through his little dog's fur, all the bravado seemed to drain out of him and I couldn't help but observe that he looked only young, and somewhat weary. I averted my eyes as he bent his head to kiss the dog between its ears. As I've said already, I've no stomach for such sights.

He was curled up in his blankets when I looked back, clutching little Luke into his chest as a child might clutch a favourite toy, and for a moment we simply watched each other like that, the rat catcher and the king, in the flickering light from the hearth.

'I'm sleepy,' said the king, at last. 'Go now and make me my trap. I want to wake up, for once, to something beautiful.'

And he closed his eyes, and fell instantly asleep.

I'm not one who expects the world to be better than it

is – not one, as I'm sure you will appreciate, to presume the existence of some magic sense of justice at work around us – and yet still I could not help but feel affronted to find the king of this most rotten state could fall asleep at nights so easily. Not so his dog, though. Little Luke's beady eyes were glinting out from within the king's grip. I wondered if he would wait like that until the morning, that small creature, holding himself as still as possible, caring only not to disturb his master.

I watched the slumbering king for a moment longer, then turned back towards the door, away from his soft breathing and the crackling warmth of the fire. I needed to gather up some branches and get somewhere well away from there, to think about the trap I was to build. I tipped the dog a nod on my way out. *Rather you than me,* was what I thought.

*

And yet, trekking back through the woods in search of somewhere good to work, I began to feel frustrated with myself. It was ridiculous to have gone to the king to voice a complaint, and to leave like that: not only hardly any further forward, but burdened with more orders to execute. King or no king, he was only a boy.

I followed the clumsy tracks I'd made earlier that evening until I was back near the palace gates, now all locked up for the night, their spiked iron bars swathed in heavy chains and padlocks. From that far away, the city beyond them seemed just a dark mass against the sky, illuminated in erratic bursts and patches – a flicker of gaslight here, the roving headlamps of a vehicle there – but I leant against the iron bars to watch it anyway, breathing the night air, so welcome in my lungs after the smoky heat of the king's dwelling. I noticed on the breeze again the faint familiar scent of rat, underlying everything like a drumbeat, and I realised I'd almost missed it back in the cabin. With this last infestation I'd grown so used to its being everywhere. I let myself relax a little, then, and as I stared out at the night-time streets I imagined to myself all the little lives crawling and scampering in the sewers and gutters. All those thousands of ordinary rodents I could catch with such relative ease, without any of the complication that seemed to vex everything I attempted in the world behind the palace gates.

I looked up then to study the rooftops, crowding over each other, irregular as rotten teeth in an old man's mouth, and I followed them along with my eyes, moving east, past the smoke pouring up from the hospital chimneys and right over to the boxy, black shapes of the old steel factories. There were no lights on in any of them, and seen from there you'd never guess that people lived in them and made them their homes.

I counted three dark roofs along, tracing my finger over

the buildings until I could pick out my own. My workshop was up there, I knew, and all my tools. Everything arranged as I liked best, waiting for me to come home and settle at my bench – with a blanket, perhaps – ready to lose myself in dreaming up a fresh creation. I was so pleased to see it there, at first. Then, though, something changed, and I had an odd experience of imagining myself up on the rooftop, standing in my old favourite spot from which to view the city, and then looking down towards the palace gates – only to see myself as I leant there, hands around the bars, looking out.

I didn't like how that felt at all, so I shook myself, and was just about to head off on my weary way again when it finally occurred to me. I say 'finally' because I suppose I had known it somewhere all along, ever since stepping into the palace through the servants' entrance by the kitchens – certainly since finding the crone at her work, feeding all of her rodents. The rats taking over the city were coming from the palace. They had to be. Nowhere else had I seen such a concentration of them, or such a vast breeding ground, so perfectly equipped for their needs. It was an outlandish, even treasonous idea, and yet now I had thought of it I couldn't ignore it. It was simply so obviously true.

Did the king know it too, I wondered, and could that be why he'd sent for me? It seemed a half-hearted effort, if that were so. Skilled in my profession as I may be, tackling the heart of a kingdom-wide infestation called for something more substantial than the simple summoning of one man. But then could I really be surprised after everything I'd seen? He had seemed to me to be a half-hearted, even a selfish, kind of king.

*

As I have said before, I usually require a sample from the pool of my prospective victims to use as a reference while I go about the business of devising a trap. And I did attempt to attract a rat or two into the clearing I chose as my workshop for the night. I didn't have my gloves with me – or any of my tins filled with my carefully concocted powders – but I found some mushrooms growing in a patch of moss at the base of a hollow tree, and I mashed them in my fingertips and spread them out upon the ground. Then, as quiet as I could possibly be, I crouched alongside the mulchy mess and waited.

The first rat to emerge from the undergrowth, poking its elongated, twitching snout from a pile of leaves a few yards from my knee, was a fine example of the palace specimens. Moonlight gleamed off his dark and glossy coat as he made straight for the mushroom bait. I lunged forward as soon as he was within my reach, but I was still sick and injured, and this rat was in his prime, sinuous and quick in spite of his massive size. He took a bite of mushroom with his raggedy fangs, then dodged from my fingers, slinking into the shadows of the trees and leaving me to land, palms-down, right in the midst of my own mushroom mixture.

Not to be deterred, I scrambled back into position. I waited again, so quiet I was hardly breathing. Crows cried out, the wind creaked in the treetops, and finally a second rat appeared, wandering towards my lure. I was poised to grab him – to smother him or break his neck – when I noticed something that unsettled me. He knew that I was there, that rat. He had seen me, I was sure of it. He could certainly smell me, at any rate. And yet as I bared my teeth and braced to spring, he made no attempt to flee. He only sniffed the air, and kept on staring – and somehow I failed to strike.

I rocked back and forth on my heels, gearing up to lunge at him and making all kinds of racket in the snow, stirring up the bracken of the forest floor, but still the creature didn't try to save himself. In fact, he wandered right up to me and sniffed my knees, and my shoes, and though he was practically offering himself to me, I have to admit I did nothing about it. It wasn't that I was feeling sentimental. It was simply that in all my years of catching rats, I'd never seen one with such flagrant disregard for the usual rules of engagement. I let him sniff around me for a little longer before shooing him back into the trees. It was foolish, probably, but I was still feeling spooked, unable to shake the image that had struck me earlier as I'd stood by the gates. It just wouldn't have felt right to me then to take something that offered itself quite so freely.

After that I knew I couldn't afford to keep waiting long by the mushroom mulch and hollow tree. It had already been a good while since I'd left the king, the night had deepened around me, and the moon had moved a way across the sky. I also didn't have any of my usual tools and materials to help me, which meant the process of building a trap would likely take far longer than I'd usually allow. I swept my eyes once more over the clearing, and, seeing no immediate sign of any other rodent there, decided it was high time I got started. As far as my prospective victims were concerned, I would have to work from memory.

It seemed a most arduous and inefficient process just at first, to be whittling at thick lengths of untreated wood with only my small penknife, and to be clambering up trees in search of materials when I was used to having at my disposal all sorts of saws and planks and blades and chemical trickery. Soon, though, as I got further into the business of construction, I found myself forgetting the limitations of my surroundings, and losing myself in the finer mechanisms and intricacies of my trap, contemplating, for instance, how I might approach the question of the lure. I didn't have my scented powders with me, and in any case, I didn't have the heart that night to tempt a creature with a mate, only to poison it instead. And then, perhaps because the king had looked so starved, or because I myself was beginning to feel hungry again, it was starting to seem like *food* might be the most appropriate bait for this latest venture of mine. I considered the matter no less carefully, I dare say, than a chef deciding on the composition of his menu, and I whistled a tune as I chipped and whittled, hammered and carved, as I plaited strings of bark up into rope, until finally the contraption was complete, and I looked up to see that it was dawn. I took off my coat and threw it over the machine. Then I lifted the shrouded whole of it up into my aching arms, and set off on my slow and painful way, back through the woods towards the cabin.

*

The smoke pouring out from the chimney was good and thick, so I assumed the king was awake. I went straight to the door, and knocked.

'Oh!' said the voice of the king from behind it. 'One moment! Do give us just one moment!'

And so I waited out there in the cold for a good five minutes, the weight of the trap dragging my arms down, practically out of their sockets – until I ran out of patience and knocked again.

'Oh!' said the king's voice again. 'Oh, do come in!'

As I struggled to reach the door handle while maintaining a firm grip on my trap, I heard him say, 'Now, little Luke, who do we think that might be?'

Eventually I got the door open. Or, that is, after a bit of fumbling the handle gave way suddenly under the pressure of my grip, causing me to trip over the threshold in a scuffle of snowflakes, tipping forward under the weight of the trap and only just keeping my footing. How reduced I was, I noticed once again, from my former health and stature. I looked up from where I'd stumbled to see a fire roaring in the grate, and then I heard the whine of little Luke behind me. I turned to the other side of the room, where I'd left the king the night before.

The blankets had been pushed away, and he was leaning against the wall with whining, wriggling little Luke clamped in his arms – and here's the thing, here's the thing that quite disgusted me. He had made himself a crown, it looked like, out of twigs and branches from the forest. Oh, but that wasn't it. He could make himself toy crowns and do himself up like that in fancy dress all he liked. What really got to me was that he'd made another, miniature crown to match his own, which he'd wedged on to the furry, stinking head of the ubiquitous little Luke.

I have made no secret of my strong belief that human beings and animals should not be made to seem alike. It was to that end, for instance, that in my healthier days, before coming to the palace, I habitually dedicated a portion of each morning to the perfecting of my posture: my insistence, for what it was worth, on my difference from everything in this world that is crawling and creeping and feral. This little show, then, of playacted affinity between man and beast struck me as being something quite perverse. And then besides all that, gripped all the while in the king's arms, Luke kept on wriggling back and forth as if trying to shake the twigs from off his head. There was something about the dog's unwillingness to play along that only made it worse.

'Good morning, Your Majesty,' I said. 'I trust that you slept well?'

'Barely,' said the king. 'That is, I barely slept at all. Little Luke here was so restless, so desperate for my attention that I could hardly catch a wink, could I now, Lucas dear?' He nuzzled his dog in that habitual way of his, their twin crowns rustling against each other as he did it. 'No, you silly one, I can hardly think what got into you. Indeed, do not let this innocent face of his deceive you. He can be quite a mischievous soul. Oh, but it is all right now, isn't it, Luke? For I have made you a crown just like my own, so there is no more need to be jealous! And he does get so terribly jealous, Mr Rat Catcher, he's almost as bad as my sister. But there we are, we are both kings now, so he is quite happy today.'

As I said, little Luke didn't look happy at all, not one bit, but I didn't think the matter worth contesting.

'I am glad to hear of it, Your Majesty,' I said, and put my trap down, still covered with my coat, in the centre of the floor, right on top of the scattered remains of the jigsaw pieces. 'You shall be pleased to know,' I told him, brushing off my hands and readjusting the coat so that it hung over the contraption at a more fetching angle, 'that for today I have devised for you a trap on the theme of woodlands, in celebration of this most charming habitat that you and your small companion have chosen as your home. Might I recommend, Your Majesty, that you look out for echoes of the smooth lines of elm in the way that I have shaped the main body of the trap? As well as for some distinctive hues of maple in the hinge? And I do hope you shall enjoy the general rustic, even pastoral, appearance of the whole. I did apply myself with diligence, Your Majesty, to the task of considering what might please you, specifically. And little Luke, of course.'

The king clapped his hands, somehow keeping a grip on Luke as he did so.

'Oh, goody,' he said. 'We *have* been looking forward to this so, have we not, little Luke, my little tiny Lucas? I, for one, simply cannot wait to see what you have devised for us, Mr Rat Catcher. Do get on with it, won't you? Don't make us wait all day.'

But this time I was determined to stand my ground. I left my coat just where it was, draped over the trap.

'First, Your Majesty, a question,' I said.

The king gave a grin that didn't extend beyond his teeth to the rest of his face. 'Well now,' he said. 'This *is* fun. A *question*? Is this part of the game? Do go ahead, Mr Rat Catcher. Your *question*, if you please?' He was mimicking my voice again – slipping in and out of it, like a ventriloquist talking to a dummy.

'Miss Ethel, Your Majesty,' I said. 'You said you had something to tell me, regarding Miss Ethel.'

'*Did* I?' said the king with widened eyes. 'But indeed, of course I did! Somehow I had quite forgotten. Oh, but I shall only tell it to you if I deem your trap worthy of that compliment you claim she gave you – what was it? *Beautiful*? Well, you can hardly blame me, Mr Rat Catcher, for wanting to find out if it really can be true. It does seem so very *unlikely*, after all.'

Luke started yapping, that horrible high-pitched sound of his that quite set my teeth on edge. It seemed the king had tightened his grip on him during that last little speech of his.

'I must insist on Your Majesty telling me now, before I show the trap.'

'How tiresome of you,' said the king. 'Is my sister really so fascinating that it cannot wait just for a moment, until after we have had our fun? Really, Mr Rat Catcher, she's not as charming as you clearly think. I can assure you, if you knew her as I do you'd never want to hear another word of her again.'

'You'll forgive me if I do insist, Your Majesty. You made me a bargain and you can see from the shape and the bulk of this object I have brought to you under my coat today that I have kept my side of it. I would like some reassurance, if you please, that you will also honour your promise.'

The king's eyes narrowed. 'Honour my promise? That is a very grand way of seeing this little game of ours, I must say. But very well, if you do *insist* upon it, I shall tell you. Only you're not allowed to blame me if it turns out you don't like it so very much after all. Because I was going to warn you, you see, about the rats. You shall have to stop catching them, I'm afraid, if you truly wish to win my sister's favour –' and here his mouth twisted up into a nasty kind of grin – 'because she loves rats, you see. Quite as much as I love my little Lucas here, although while for me there is but one little Luke, she has room in her heart for every single one of them. Oh, but there's no need to look so murderous about it, Mr Rat Catcher. Every word I say is true, I can assure you! Since she was a child the rats have been her only companions – aside, that is, from that horrible, half-witted mother of hers, and she can barely count as company. But she never played with any of her toys, my sister, and she refused to play with me, certainly, whenever I was brought to her. She wouldn't even talk. She'd just snarl or even scratch at me if ever I tried to start a game with her, and then stare out of the window until I was taken off again. Oh, but the rats, now – she would *always* play with them. It was as if she had some kind of affinity with them, one even might say . . . which is why, Mr Rat Catcher, it seems so very *unlikely* to me that she should admire your trap so much. Do correct me if you think I'm wrong, but I cannot help but conclude that she must have been *lying* to you. Oh, but there's no need to look so foul about it.' He waved a hand as if dismissing the whole matter. 'You can show *me* your trap now, and perhaps *I* really shall think it beautiful, and then you shall have the praise of one of us, at least! Go on, Mr Rat Catcher, show it now, do.'

He hoisted little Luke up in his arms, and clapped his hands again. I found that I could hardly breathe.

'It's cruel of you,' I said, at last, 'to say such things about Miss Ethel.'

'I don't care,' said the king. 'I've told you all I had to say – now it is your turn to *honour your promise*. Now *you* must fulfil your end of the bargain.'

Well, I could hardly order my thoughts, especially with little Luke there, still making such a racket. So instead of coming back with some clever riposte to show his strange story hadn't troubled me at all, I merely shook my head and walked around, closer to the fire, until I was standing right behind my trap.

I took a breath, reminded myself of my resolve back in the forest . . . and then I reached down, seized the top of my draped coat, and whipped it away. There was a gasp from the king, and I looked up to see his face. Not so cocky or so spiteful now. Like a frightened child, he seemed, in that moment, and I felt a thrill go through me to see it. He soon rearranged his features, but he knew that I had seen. I limped out from behind the trap.

'Note the detail on this central curving structure, here,' I said. 'I have carved into the wood an accentuation of the original bark patterns. Simply for aesthetic value, you understand, to contribute to the woodland theme, to the pastoral refrain, and to give to the whole something more of the appearance of a tree. I have also carved into the wood *here*, and *here*, and *here* –' I crouched down by my trap and gestured to the places – 'some little notches and grooves. *Paw-holds*, if you will, spaced apart at exactly the optimum distance for rats the size and scale of those to be found within your palace, Majesty, and designed to make the route up the trunk a little easier and more appealing, if you will, though they are of course mostly a formality, for although your palace rats are somewhat fat, they should

still require no help where the matter of climbing is concerned.' I grinned at him and ran my hand up my trap,
coming to the branches of the tree. 'These wooden stars
you see here are a version of my signature . . . and *here*,
my king, we have the finale.'

'A bird's nest?' said the king, sounding not entirely
comfortable – and how I relished the edge of uncertainty
in his voice.

'A bird's nest, yes,' I said. 'Well spotted, Your Majesty.
Also with a medley of woodland mushrooms, crushed and
laid out on the bed of it, to further contribute to the delicious aromatic wafts of edibles and treats.'

'I see,' said the king, sounding, if I may say it, a little
strangled.

'You will note, here, a small platform, skirting round
the nest, Your Majesty?'

'Yes, Mr Rat Catcher, I see it.'

'I have filed and treated the wood for a distance all
around this section of the tree to make this platform the
necessary final step before making the leap into the nest.'

'What happens when they reach the platform, Mr Rat
Catcher?'

'What happens when they reach the platform?' I repeated back at him. 'Ah, I'm very glad you asked. For *this*
is what happens, Your Majesty.' And I patted the uppermost mechanism of the trap. 'The weight of the rat on the

platform triggers this crane-like section of the mechanism to come into play, causing this noose of knotted bark to sweep along from underneath – you see? Just here? – and to tighten right at the point, quite precisely, where my calculations tell me it shall find the sleek, plump neck of our dear rodent, whereupon the platform, of course, shall fall away, and lo – Mr Rat has hanged himself.'

'I see,' said the king again. 'But, Mr Rat Catcher, surely that means this trap will work only to catch one rat? Which is not really very efficient, when you consider it properly, now, is it?'

But I was too absorbed in my demonstration to pay him much attention.

'Now, if you will allow me, Your Majesty,' I said, 'the finishing touch.' And I reached into the little bird's nest at the top of my tree, took out one of the eggs, cracked it against the side of the platform, then broke it over all the other eggs and mushrooms in the nest – quite in the manner of a fancy French cook, was my idea.

'To increase the pungency, Your Majesty,' I said.

I did not, however, have long to enjoy the pleasure of the moment, for as I broke the shell of that little egg, Luke began to yap again. I had momentarily forgotten him, it has to be said. Something, I dare say, about the authority in my voice as I had explained my trap had quieted him. At any rate, I'd been too preoccupied to feel vexed by him. Which was why, perhaps, I was somewhat slow to respond when he wriggled free from his master's arms to bound across the room towards my tree. The king was still staring at the nest and so he too did not react as quickly as he might have done.

'Luke,' he said, when his slow brain had caught up with the progress of events. '*Luke,*' he cried. But still he only stood there and gawped while little Luke scampered up the trunk, knocking aside my wooden stars as he made his way. And my lord, it must have been a month or more since that dog had had a proper meal. I have rarely seen a creature charge into a trap with quite such desperation.

'*Lucas!*' the king cried out again. But it was only when his dog had reached the platform that the king's limbs caught up with the rest of him and he dashed after his poor, precious pet. It was, though, as I have said before, quite a large space, and by the time the king had reached us – by the time, that is, he had propelled himself to stand alongside the dog, the trap and me – it was too late, and Luke was all caught up in the rope, his neck quite snapped, choking out his last.

The king let out a most unearthly wail. It even got me wondering – if only for a second, you understand – if I'd made a huge mistake. I didn't have long to consider it, though, because before I knew what was occurring he'd launched himself upon my trap, knocking it to the floor and sending little Luke a-swinging, the bird's nest a-flying, all the eggs a-rolling, and the mushroom mash a-pouring out on to the cabin floor. And then the king was crouched and tugging at the length of knotted bark around the neck of little Luke, trying to untie the rope and making the most ungodly noises – the most hideous sounds I've heard a fellow human being make, and that's saying something, given what goes on in the part of the city I inhabit. It was quite remarkable to see the king reduced like that. Not a sight I'd ever have expected to witness within my lifetime, let alone to see and know that such a thing had been brought about by my own hand.

'His neck is broken,' I said, at last. 'It would be kinder now to let him die.'

But that only set the king off on his shrieking and his sobbing and his tugging at the rope again.

'My god,' I said, limping a circle round the sorry mess of him. 'You don't half make a lot of noise, do you? But you should think, Your Majesty. There's an infestation out beyond your gates, spreading from your very palace halls, filling the city streets with sickness and disease. There are even people who are dying out there because of it. Everyone frightened and desperate, with whispers of plague wherever you turn. Do you make this kind of noise for them? Do all those human beings merit an equivalent cacophony to the one provoked by the loss of this one pathetic little piece of vermin?' I grabbed the king by the collar of his shirt, dragged him off the twitching tiny body and pulled him up so that we were almost nose-to-nose. 'Of course not,' I said. 'You don't even notice them.'

'But he's not vermin,' said the king, sounding hoarse. 'He's a living, thinking – he's—' He broke off, coughed, cleared his throat and looked right up at me with an odd expression on his face, like that of a man genuinely trying to explain something very important. 'He's not vermin. He's Lucas. And he's so small and kind and tender, and when he's with me, somehow, I never have bad dreams.'

I let go of the king's collar and he dropped straight down to the floor, just like a bag of bones.

'Pathetic,' I said, and turned my back on him, limping off to stare into the fire.

We spent a few moments like that in relative quiet. At first there was a fair amount of snivelling and whimpering from the king behind me – and the last choking sounds from little Luke, of course – until they both fell silent, leaving me with only the crackling of the flames to listen to. I calmed my beating heart with a few slow breaths.

'You did it deliberately,' said the king, behind me, after a time. 'You made that trap deliberately for Luke, didn't you?'

'I don't know,' I said into the fire.

'I think you must really be a monster,' said the king,

and his voice sounded different, more like he'd finally pulled himself together and had got up from the floor, from all that absurd hunching over his dying pet. I should have turned to look at him – I know I should have done – to show him I wasn't ashamed of myself, or afraid of him at all, and yet somehow I couldn't do it. I sensed him stepping closer, so quiet there with his bare feet, but still I turned my face away.

'But why would you do that, Mr Rat Catcher? I told the truth about my sister, I really did. I thought that you had come to help us.'

'I cannot say, Your Majesty,' I said, still averting my gaze.

'Poor little Luke,' the king continued. 'He never hurt a living soul in all his life. And now –' the king's voice trembled – 'I simply cannot think what I shall do without him.'

And I'm not proud of what I said next. In fact I'm not sure why I said it at all.

'I apologise, Your Majesty,' I said.

Then I sensed a flash of movement from behind me, and I twisted round to see the king swinging a long piece of wood through the fire, flames dancing up along the length of it, the top part of my mechanism for the hangman's noose, it seemed, now torn loose and set completely ablaze. I tried to leap out of its way, but I had frostbite nibbling at my toes and poison still washing back and forth inside my veins, and all sorts of aches and pains besides. In short, I was too slow. The flames on the end of the stick made contact with the sleeve of my shirt just in the moment before they licked up the other side of it towards the king's hands, and he cried out and hurled the whole burning thing away from him, back into the hearth.

I watched him check the skin of his palms for burns as fire chased its way down my sleeve, down my trouser leg and across my chest – and I continued to watch as the king looked up and stared at me with those wide eyes of his, which seemed to suggest it was all an innocent, honest mistake – until finally the pain bloomed, and my awareness of the smell of burning flesh sent me sprinting for the door.

I launched myself headlong into the snow as soon as I reached it, fire and water hissing in the moment of contact, and I rolled myself over and over on the ground, finding more snow, more new territory on which to put out the flames. I never thought I'd feel so grateful for this endless winter that we live in. Then, thank god, at last I saw the flames were out, though my skin was still scorching hot and sticky, melded with my rags of clothing. I picked myself up off the ground – that was enough of rolling in the dirt – and, not pausing to examine the extent of my injuries, I headed for the lake.

I made my way through the trees erratically, crashing into trunks and branches and feeling twigs dragging over my raw scalp, until at last I made it to the palace drive. By god, then did I run, sprinting back the way I'd come not so very long ago, after saying goodnight to Ethel. At last I reached the spot where we'd sat together under the stars with our glasses of wine – and how beautiful she'd looked in the moonlight with that fur around her shoulders – but I didn't pause to savour the memory. Rather, I pitched myself forward, leaping like the desperate creature I was, out on to the surface of the lake. The parts of my skin that made contact with the ice seemed to cry out quite as loudly as the king had done over his ridiculous dog, and then the ice cracked underneath me with a sound like breaking bones, and I fell right through it, into the water below.

Sinking, floating down – it was excruciating at first; the cold seeming to batter at my stomach and inside my skull – until eventually, quite suddenly, it was bearable, and I opened my eyes and saw the ice above me like a hard, translucent ceiling. And then I looked around, and saw too that there was nothing in the lake at all that could trouble or disturb me, because nothing lives in a place as hostile and as harsh as that. There were only stones, right at the bottom. I propelled myself towards them, and the water felt almost pleasant on my skin as I moved through it, soothing my burns. I stayed down there for as long as I could possibly hold my breath.

When I broke the surface again, bursting back up through that little gap in the ice I had made in falling through, I blinked and shook my head from side to side until my eyes felt clear. I was in such a bad state that I was too frightened to rub them, too scared to touch any part of myself in case the heat from my hands set the burning feeling off again, or parts of my damaged skin simply fell off into my fingers. When I could see again I stared up a moment at the sky, and then paddled myself around in my little enclosure of water until I was facing back down the palace drive. The gates were far away now, right at the bottom, but standing open once again. And there was my city, too, still beckoning, still festering beyond.

I splashed back round to face the palace, and realised that for the first time, perhaps, I was seeing it truly as it was. I had never liked it much, but it seemed that finally there was not even a hint left of awe, or fear, or bitterness, or even curiosity to colour my view of it as I studied it from the lake. It was as if the fire had scoured all of that away, and instead I saw simply the core of the infestation: all those rows of fangs in amongst the columns and the colonnades; all the hungry rodent faces lurking behind the gargoyles on the battlements . . . and all the piles of fat, cooling rodent bodies lying in heaps at the feet of velvet curtains and gilded doorways, in the places where I'd set my trails of Emerald Dust. Then I noticed some movement from one of the windows off to the left of the building, and a curtain twitched aside.

It was Ethel, in the window. As composed and as perfect as when I'd seen her last, that night on the banks of the lake. An image came into my mind unbidden as I stared up at her, of her as a young child, left alone in the empty nursery, with only the rats for company. Did it have the stamp of truth to it, I wondered. And could it, then, be that the king had sent for me merely out of spite towards his sister, and not out of any real desire to put an end to the infestation at all? *I thought that you had come to help us*, he had said, back at the cabin. What had he really meant by that?

She didn't notice me at first, as she looked out across the grounds. But then, of course, she did. She gave a start back from the window and disappeared from view. I wondered if that would be the last I'd see of her but she soon returned, with that mother of hers at her side. The two of them stared down at me, Ethel's delicate features and the crone's distorted into matching grotesque looks that showed as plain as day their horror at seeing me returned to them like this, so soon after sending me packing to the realms of the dead.

Fixing my gaze on her as steadily as I could manage while still treading water, I twisted my ragged mouth up into a grin, and then I raised a hand and waved.

Accelerate!

It was the fault of the intern. Or at least it began when the intern brought me a latte I hadn't asked for. I'd arrived in London a few months previously and I'd never tasted coffee much before. I say *much* . . . I'd tried it a couple of times. Of course I'd been curious as a teenager and taken a few tentative eye-watering sips in the hope I'd appear sophisticated and mature. Of course I'd drunk the occasional whipped-cream sugar-laden Starbucks Mochaccino in my Saturdays wandering the vacuous halls of our local shopping centre or walking back and forth from the library – but for the most part I'd never understood the bitterness of coffee or the intensity or the way every mouthful seemed to send my heart tick-tick-ticking faster at the same time as making the colours of everything brighter and the edges sharper as if some elf were messing about with the levels in the Photoshop program of my brain and pushing the contrast slider up and up and up.

But to get back to the intern and the latte he brought me. It was my first job out of uni and I'll admit that in those early days I didn't understand the work. Didn't understand it not only in literal terms (my brain was scrambled daily

– I'd said on my CV I was adept at Microsoft Excel and while I hadn't meant to lie I'd certainly misunderstood the program's capabilities) but also on a more existential level. What the company did seemed interesting and important but in a hypothetical scenario in which I had to explain in simple terms what my role within it was – or even for that matter what the company's role within wider society might be – I was afraid that I would struggle. So as the intern approached I have to say that I was feeling somewhat insecure and even unsure of whether I merited the work-station I'd managed to grab for myself that morning in the ruthless hot-desking scrum and I therefore accepted the coffee with nothing more than a simple nod. My intention being to seem so authoritative and *au fait* with the office routine that the whole thing was hardly worthy of comment.

I should say at this point – I have always been wary of any substance that has an effect on the chemical processes of the mind. Alcohol I only drink tentatively and I would never touch any more powerful drug. I am no risk-taker and I've certainly worked too hard all my life (my CV is close to perfect excepting that overstatement of my acquaintance with Microsoft Excel) to throw any of that to the winds. I do believe that whenever you are led to gamble – the house will always win.

And yet still eager to show the intern I belonged where

I was I took a large gulp of the hot liquid in front of me. And perhaps my tastebuds had been altered by the constant exposure to the poor air quality of the city because though my stomach churned – affronted by this harsh assault – I realised at once that this was something quite compelling.

I looked about myself as it diffused its way through my system. I surveyed the desk and computer terminal in front of me. I studied the stacked-up papers I knew I had to do something about (though what that something was had been made sadly unclear to me when I'd been handed them that morning). I swept my gaze over the open-plan office floor with its pot plants and water coolers and corkboards all pinned with hundreds of bright and incomprehensible charts . . . and all at once I began to feel more comfortable in this new world I'd found myself in. I began to feel almost at home.

I set to work and accomplished more in the next two hours than I could remember doing before in any equivalent period of my life. It didn't matter that I didn't understand the work and still couldn't fathom what it was for. It was easy when you simply *did* it and didn't question it. I smiled at my colleagues and even joked and chatted as I ticked off task after task on my list. I blithely ignored the intern. And though the coffee stubbornly refused to settle and churned away in the depths of my digestive system it felt good to be at work and in London. It felt exactly – at last – the way I'd always hoped it would.

*

One latte led to another and then eventually to a cappuccino and I carried on like that until I was introduced to the flat white – the cappuccino's more sophisticated cousin. I liked how they were made stronger and with fewer concessions to simple childish crutches like the frothed milk and the layer of chocolate sprinkles.

Before long I was drinking coffee when nobody was watching. On weekends for instance I would march through London's streets taking galvanising sips from a warm takeaway cup in my hands. I found that such an activity did wonders for my mood and somehow enhanced my fundamental sense of purpose. Coffee synchronised my internal metronome with the rhythms of the city and I felt as if with the first sip of each day a switch in my head was located and flicked that allowed me to accomplish in less than an hour what most normal people would take a whole day to complete.

I watched my fellow coffee-drinkers with curiosity – did they also develop this strange ability when they swallowed the delicious fluid? I observed carefully and concluded it couldn't be possible. The general discourse surrounding coffee in our society was too concerned with notions of leisure for such a thing to be feasible. The type of sped-up living I was experiencing was in no way appropriate for a Sunday morning at the kitchen table flipping through the newspapers while ignoring the headlines and only idly reading the lifestyle supplements. Even to maintain a relaxed posture seated in only one location for more than a matter of minutes was starting to seem to me laughably absurd.

I watched my colleagues at the office and realised that these older men in their static-infused polyester suits no longer seemed sophisticated to me. They were so *slow*. Lumpen and clumsy in both their movements and their thoughts. And they made mistakes. Countless small errors – the misuse of an apostrophe in an email or the casual placement of a document in a cabinet under the wrong file divider. Needless to say I noticed them all and corrected them so quickly no one was even aware I was doing it because it wasn't credit or praise that I wanted. I didn't care any more whether the boss liked me as he was just another polyester-clad slug eking his way through the day. It was simply that I couldn't stand the fundamental lack of elegance in their mistakes and had to put it right.

That inelegance irked me more than almost anything else. The speeding up of my internal world had led to a sort of streamlining efficiency in everything I accomplished. It was that old maxim of William Morris's – *Have nothing in your house that you do not know to be useful or believe to be beautiful* – except I applied it not just to my house but to my thoughts and my actions and while I could certainly see a number of like-minded individuals around me as I went about the city I couldn't help notice that by no means everybody seemed to be able to bring themselves in tune with this more effective way of being. It dawned on me that switching into life's fast lane like this was a particular and enviable capability. A kind of super-power if you will.

*

I met Annalise in an Italian restaurant (I had long since abandoned cooking as an unnecessary waste of time). Annalise with the terrible memory. Annalise who I recognised as trouble or something like it from the moment I looked up from my *saltimbocca alla Romana* just in time to catch her start singing from the makeshift stage in the corner and for our eyes to meet across the room through that sea of pepper-grinders and birthday party tables and old-couple tables and awkward-first-date tables in that specific way that always seems to happen in movies but never so much in real life. There she was with the words of 'Hallelujah' hanging on her lips unhurried – a still point in the chaos.

The thing about Annalise I noticed even from that very first time I heard her sing was how different this specific quality of stillness she possessed was from the other kinds of slow behaviour that so frustrated me in my colleagues and in the tourists or old people who persisted in using public transport during rush hour. She wasn't sluggish and she wasn't clumsy. She wasn't at all inefficient. She was just perfectly comfortable both in her own skin and in the seconds and minutes and hours her body occupied.

As a result she was one of the most beautiful singers I've witnessed. The beginning and end of 'Hallelujah' for instance were the beginning and end of the universe for her once she'd started on it and something about that – the way she inhabited every line fully and equally with a complete lack of any sense that she might be rushing to get to the end of the song – made an audience believe her utterly. More than just believe. *Became complicit* seems more accurate. Or in any case that was how I felt watching her there. And I didn't even like 'Hallelujah'. It was a disappointingly obvious choice but still I was hypnotised – not by the words or the melody but by this peculiar alchemy she managed to exercise over my perception of the passage of time when she sang. It was a force and an influence completely opposite to my personal mission of getting my money's worth out of every passing second – and needless to say I was hooked.

She came over to my table after she'd finished singing – clearly not in any rush to get there as she stopped to talk to every person who congratulated her and thanked her for the music on the way. Indeed her progress towards me was so gradual I started to wonder if I'd misunderstood our moment of electric eye contact completely and she wasn't even on her way at all. It was all I could do to sit still and wait. I wanted to spring up and dash over to her or give the whole thing up for lost and just leave. I fiddled with my fork the candlestick my coffee cup (I'd moved on to drinking straight espresso by then) and I tapped my nails against the side of a bottle of chilli oil. Then I rummaged in my bag for my laptop and opened it up to start some freelance work I'd taken on – just some copyediting stuff nothing too remarkable I suppose I was just bored by my job not getting enough of a challenge and needing to fill up the new free hours I had since I was getting everything out of the way so quickly. I was well into the eighth page of the document by the time she finally appeared in front of me.

'Are you OK?' she said. 'I just . . . saw you here all by yourself. You looked so tired.'

I ordered us a bottle of wine. I'm usually more circumspect with alcohol but faced with Annalise it seemed the occasion merited it and I was seized with sudden recklessness. I told her to sit down.

As we talked I noticed her actions and decision making were even slower than that of a bog-standard human being. That is to say she was frequently almost at a standstill pausing in conversation in the middle of a thought to sip her wine and take a long slow inhale and close her eyes as she waited for the flavour to die on her lips. Except that was just it. She wasn't waiting for the flavour to die. That's what I would have been doing – mentally rushing on to the moment when it would be time for me to take another gulp and so hurrying the whole process on that way. I suppose she was what all those trite time-wasting lifestyle magazines would call *living in the moment*. She hardly seemed to speculate about the future and she never talked about the past – something that is not surprising to me now that I know more about her appalling memory – and she seemed perfect in her actions not because they were superbly time-saving and energy-efficient like my own but because they were very contentedly leading absolutely nowhere. They had no purpose or agenda beyond themselves and so occupied space and time with absolute elegance.

'You're the most beautiful person I've ever met,' I told her that first evening after my half-bottle of wine.

'Really?' she said. 'Because I thought . . . or at least it

seemed just there like you were . . . I don't know. Like you were angry with me, or something.'

'I could never be angry with you,' I told her and reached for her hand across the tablecloth.

*

I was already bored with so many of the songs she sang before I even met her and she never tried to learn anything new with any strategy or effort. Sometimes in the mornings when I was dressed for work and making the first coffee of the day (I had long since invested in a Nespresso machine) she would shamble out of bed still in pyjamas and then stretching out her limbs in unconscious contentment at the simple way she inhabited all the corners of her body she would pad into the living room pick up her guitar (both she and the guitar lived at mine within a month of my meeting her as I didn't see the point in simply dating for ages in a non-committal way and then also the thing about Annalise's extreme present-ness was that it seemed she frequently didn't get round to organising anywhere to live and was usually in effect rather homeless) and she would yawn and pluck a few chords and then finally begin to sing something different. Except she'd never stick at it. She never learnt any new song through to its conclusion because the second it ceased bringing her uncomplicated pleasure she stopped. Simple as that. I both loved her for it and was appalled. Why would she start learning something if she was never going to finish the process? It was such a flagrant waste of time I couldn't help but consider it quite spectacular.

Perhaps the contrast in our values and our tempos threw the nature of my sped-up living into sharper relief because the longer Annalise and I lived together the better I felt I was beginning to understand my own abilities. Although I'd fallen into a pattern of consuming between six and eight double espressos by the afternoon I was also beginning to question whether this power I had to accelerate through the few hours the universe allotted to each particular day was entirely caffeine dependent. The switch in my head that yes admittedly coffee had been the first thing to flick into the 'on' position seemed ever more easily locatable for me. I couldn't help but feel that with a little more practice I might – if hypothetically I wanted to – discard the coffee altogether and truly *understand* how I could speed up my internal timescape independently.

Although occasionally usually while lying in bed with Annalise I did wonder: in accelerating like this was I really cramming more living experience into the allotted hours of my life? Or was I just hurtling towards the end of my own personal timeline with blithe alacrity? Did you have to die young to live fast? It seemed an absurd equation. Real life does not feel like fertile territory for such neo-Faustian pacts. But still I wondered about the trade-off. It seemed too good to be true that you could get more life just by living more quickly – and you'll remember I'm wary of gambles. I never forget that the house always wins. I wanted to know what Annalise thought. I regularly wondered aloud on this theme and begged her to give me some kind of answer. It was lucky she had such a terrible memory or I'm sure she would have become bored with me.

That was a strange thing – Annalise's famous memory. It may have kept her free of hauntings from the past but as time went on with the two of us together I started to feel haunted myself not by ghosts of things remembered but by a particular kind of uncertainty. I was always looking over my shoulder to check whether the things I thought had occurred had really truly happened. She never forgot the lyrics to her songs but she forgot our conversations all the time. She forgot acquaintances and sequences of events that led up to what were for me significant moments – and then she forgot those too. She forgot how we met and where. She forgot where we were the first time we kissed. And yet still for someone so forgetful she was surprisingly constant in her feelings. She told me she loved me and I believed her every time. Perhaps she didn't need an accumulation of shared memories to base that conviction on. Perhaps the present impulse was enough. I prayed it would continue to be so and gathered up our memories on my own – storing away for the two of us what slipped her mind so easily.

*

Our lifestyles became increasingly incompatible. Annalise lived in the still moments of individual songs and lyric poems and I was now moving too quickly to think comfortably even in prose and was needing to inhabit an even faster-moving medium. We decided to take a weekend away to work on our problems.

```
1 EXT. THE WOODS IN SOMERSET - 4.36 P.M.

It's a glorious afternoon - dappled sunlight
... all the rest of it. EVGENY (ME that is)
and ANNALISE (HER obviously) are out walking.

                    EVGENY
    What do you think about when we're
    walking like this? What goes through
    your mind?

                    ANNALISE
    I ... I don't know, really. I just
    ... well I suppose - this is going
    to sound really funny - but I suppose
    I'm thinking about the smell.
```

                    EVGENY

The smell?

                    ANNALISE

Yeah. I'd say so. I live for
this, y'know? It just smells so
... earthy and fresh and ... it's
not like being in the city. The air's
a different thing out here. It's like
here ... here we can really be free.

                    EVGENY

We're free in the city. We're free
wherever we are.

                    ANNALISE

But out here we can really *feel* it.

She PAUSES and thinks for a few beats.
I - EVGENY that is - am - is - visibly
impatient to hear the verbal manifestation
of her burgeoning thought. He keeps glancing
sideways to scrutinise her face in little
glances snatched between strides.

                    ANNALISE

And I don't know if that's true,
that we're really free in the city.

I mean, you're always working, aren't
you? It's not like ... well. Hardly
any of your time belongs to you.

                    EVGENY
I like my work Annalise. It keeps my
mind quiet.

PAUSE. They walk.

                    ANNALISE
Is it not quiet now?

                    EVGENY
Is what not quiet?

                    ANNALISE
Your mind.

                    EVGENY
Sorry. I was on another planet.

PAUSE.

                    ANNALISE
So ... what is it you think about
then, Evgeny? When we're walking like
this?

                    EVGENY

I - well. I plan. I think of
everything I want to do and then what
really needs to be prioritised and
focused on in the next week. Then I
think about what available time slots
I have left to play with. And then I
allocate things to those time slots.
I do that - and I worry.

                    ANNALISE

What about?

                    EVGENY

I don't know. The situation in the
Middle East. Terrorism. The tiny
potentiality that there's just no
point in anyone planning anything
because we'll all be dead next
week. I try not to. It's just like
background radio noise - it doesn't
occupy too much of my attention.

ANNALISE takes my - EVGENY'S - hand.

                    ANNALISE

You can't worry about stuff like
that. You'd go crazy.

                    EVGENY

    I know. Of course I know. Worrying's
    a waste of time.

2 INT. THE HOTEL BEDROOM - 11.42 P.M.

Generic standard-issue IKEA fittings and
furniture. EVGENY and ANNALISE are lying side
by side in the dark.

                    EVGENY

    Annalise?

                    ANNALISE

    Mmm?

                    EVGENY

    Do you ever feel sometimes like
    you're two people? Like you're two
    people at once and you're inhabiting
    one of yourselves while observing
    what the other one is doing over
    there from a detached kind of
    perspective? And then all at once
    you're the other one looking out
    through those eyes from a distance
    at the self you were convinced you

were primarily inhabiting just a
few seconds before. And then you're
suddenly not sure at all which one
of the two you are - and then you
start to suspect that you are in
fact neither and that there's a third
version of yourself sitting detached
from both of the other two and
assessing these thoughts as you think
them. And then you start to wonder
if that's the one you really are or
if you're still just watching him
from a distance - considering him as
he considers the aspects of you.

Long PAUSE. ANNALISE shifts around on the bed
to look at EVGENY.

                    ANNALISE
     I'm sorry Evgeny. I can honestly say
     I've never felt like that.

                    EVGENY
     Oh. Right. Fine.

                    ANNALISE
     Sometimes ... sometimes I wonder if
     you're really here with me at all,

or off in your head somewhere –
making plans or solving puzzles or
... I don't know. I don't know what
more than half of you is thinking,
most of the time.

EVGENY

So you do understand what I mean.

PAUSE during which he stares at her anxiously
– why won't she hurry up and answer?

ANNALISE

Yes, I suppose I do. I've just never
felt that way myself, is all.

EVGENY

Right.

PAUSE.

EVGENY (CON'T)

I was thinking. Earlier. In the
woods. That I should maybe be setting
aside a few chunks of protected time
– perhaps even a few slots every
week – during which I make an effort
to be focused on only the unfolding
present. On the sights and sounds and

smells ... Really it was when you
were talking about the smell that I—

ANNALISE

The smell?

EVGENY

Yes. It was when you started talking
about the smell and your answer
seemed just so alien to me that I
thought—

ANNALISE

What smell?

EVGENY

You don't ... of course. Of course
you don't remember.

PAUSE.

ANNALISE

I'm sorry.

EVGENY

It's OK.

Long PAUSE.

226

> ANNALISE
>
> I love you.

> EVGENY
>
> I love you too.

Silence.

3 EXT. THE RIVERBANK - 10.23 A.M.

> ANNALISE
>
> (She's angry, this doesn't happen
> often.)
> ... look outside of your mind, just
> for one minute, Evgeny. Look at all
> the things that surround you. Look
> up, look out of your own eyes. Look
> at those birds, or, I don't know,
> that plant, or - or at me. Look at
> me, Evgeny. Properly. Please.

But EVGENY - I that is - just keep staring
ahead. I've stopped walking and so has she
but I don't turn from the path as I say this
next part.

> EVGENY
>
> Why? Why should I look at you

```
        Annalise? Why should I look at you
        when you won't remember whether I did
        or not by the evening?

    Now I turn to her - or turn on her you could
    say.

                EVGENY (CON'T)
        Why is your memory so bad anyway?
        What did you do to yourself that
        it completely deserted you? Did you
        smoke so much weed that it just
        disappeared? Is it drugs? Is it
        ketamine or coke or do you just drink
        too much? Or is it none of that at
        all and you simply just aren't paying
        attention?
```

We both ended that weekend knowing each of us was more alone in the world of our partnership than we'd ever considered before. I drove back to London. Annalise took the train.

*

I was feeling lonely and contrite and also slightly disturbed by the realisation I'd had lying next to Annalise on our weekend away: that most of the time now my mind was processing so many things at once that I felt like at least five people – none of which I was sure was a primary version of me that I could relax into inhabiting and feel certain of being. Part of me was for instance heartbroken over Annalise while the rest of me was alienated from the feeling – each worry or concern outsourced to a different segment of self to maximise efficiency. So I cut down on the espresso and scheduled one yoga class every Friday evening after I finished in the office before I got started on my freelance commitments. Through a mixture of ujjayi breathing and decaf lattes I managed to think my way back into a kind of prose.

After two weeks of not talking Annalise and I took a walk by the Thames to discuss our troubles. It turned out she couldn't remember why we'd argued. She'd reinvented our backstory in her head and shot it down as something insignificant – which is what it seemed to her since that was how she had manufactured that false memory to be. Of course she couldn't understand why we couldn't simply reconcile. I tied myself in knots explaining it. I felt insane telling this beautiful woman I loved that we couldn't be together because of some slippery past she had so loose a grip on that even I was starting to doubt everything had happened in the way I remembered.

I ran away from her that evening. All the way down the Southbank and into the BFI bar where I ordered a double shot espresso because who cared about cutting down any more and connected to the wifi and looked up what happened around the city on a Wednesday evening – Wednesday being the night I traditionally reserved for Annalise. I booked and paid for a term of Wednesday night Taekwondo classes and felt instantly triumphant before knocking back the coffee I'd ordered and leaving the realm of uncomplicated prose behind again as my internal world began clattering along too fast even to be in tune with the syncopated rhythms and jump cuts of a movie. I left linearity behind I left logic behind and as I dashed around the city going to work changing tubes answering emails on my phone checking the BBC news checking the news on Al Jazeera checking the *New York Times* checking WhatsApp Facebook Messenger Instagram Twitter emails again BBC news again getting to work and more emails and phone calls and jobs to see off and data to enter and copy to write and statements to approve and invoices to log and colleagues to greet and coffee coffee coffee to drink my sense of self coalesced only very occasionally in the disconnected isolated lists and thoughts I jotted down for myself using the Notes app on my phone in some instinctual bid to log how I felt and so keep some kind of track of my scattered identity as I chased myself around from commitment to commitment.

Accelerate!

coffee
toothpaste
binbags
milk

there should be book trolleys on trains. with
bespoke recommendations

oatcakes
coffee
fairy dishwasher things
rubber gloves
hand cream
ibuprofen

I'm not sure I enjoy taekwondo. I'm starting to
doubt my decision.

my head is so filled with noise I can hardly bear to
exist

My heart's a mess. Desecrated. A flat in
the aftermath of a mysterious police raid in
a substandard BBC TV drama. Stuff strewn
everywhere and removed from context.

I'm sick of being torn apart by uncertainty in love
when the whole world seems to be ending.

kitchen roll
bread
margarine
soap
shower stuff
cereal bars
eggs
coffee

It's such a beautiful day here on this train. I think you've just got to take that for what it is as opposed to a sign that the world isn't in self-destruct.

why are there still no book trolleys on trains? what is it that the rest of you are all doing? am I the only one in this country who ever has any new ideas at all?

*

As those collected relics stored in my Notes app reveal I finally dragged myself out of the whirlpool of London and got on a train. Or part of me did in any case. The other six parts as I was certain there must at least be by now considering that when I looked back at those notes they all seemed to be written by different people were . . . somewhere else. Even though they were technically part of me I still couldn't tell what they were currently doing. They were up in the sky for all I knew and I didn't care I'd lost track of them.

This I saw must be the trade-off of the Faustian pact. You didn't die young necessarily because you lived fast. You just divided yourself into pieces and pieces of pieces – and then lost track of most of those as they spun around so fast that they careered off their own orbits and got lost and irrevocable in some nonspecific ether of notional productivity. Maybe one of those selves was with Annalise right now . . . oh but I was the embodiment of divided attention and the self on the train couldn't be bothered to think about Annalise any more. He was just happy to look out of the window at the clouds and the sheep and the rolling green fields. And he – I – the Evgeny on the train – cheerily thanked the lady pushing the refreshments trolley as she topped up my coffee while another part of me gloomily reflected that if this dispersal of self was the inevitable consequence of cramming more life into your limited allotted time then the house really does always win – a conclusion that then distracted another part of me from the survey he happened to be filling out on my phone about the service I'd received from the automated voice that had helped me pay my gas bill as he began to feel insufferably smug for always being correct about that fundamental law of gambling. I tried my best to align my mood with that part of myself for the moment seeing as he did after all seem by far the most jovial – and I laughed as I looked out of the window.

I got off the train at Bath Spa – the closest station to where Annalise and I had attempted to have our romantic weekend away – and struck out straight into the woods to where Annalise had been so taken by the scent of the clear air. And once I was there I stood and inhaled and inhaled through my nostrils and still every single part of myself that I retained some hold over felt nothing. And though part of me was entertained by the ironic gulf between my physical situation and the *New Yorker* article about ideal relationships he seemed to be scanning and scrolling through as we walked the rest of me found itself bored with the scenery as I made my way back through the trees. I took a turning off the road hoping for better things and stepped out of the woods into a field high on the side of a hill.

*

It was as he – I – Evgeny was heading down this hill and striking back out towards the station according to what the most countryside-savvy fragment of myself judged would be the best balance between the most direct and most entertainingly varied routes – that something swept into my eyeline and demanded my attention: a pattern. A perfect solved puzzle, airborne and fluid. Hundreds of wings moving in synchrony back and forth like a scattering of iron filings laid out before a magnet or like a shoal of fish or like a drop of mercury prodded back and forth on a bench. Something perplexing intellectually but which still in my heart and my gut made a perfect kind of sense. It was what I am now aware is conventionally referred to as a murmuration of starlings. And if you haven't seen one of these then YouTube it now. The magic is all in the way that it – they – move – or moves. You see I'm still not sure which grammatical construction is the more appropriate and that's part I think of what struck me as so beautiful when this murmuration shimmered into the sky up ahead of me. Or in fact don't YouTube it. If you've got time then get on a train and find one – how's that for me learning something? Anyway this murmuration – it moved as if there was some conspiracy of knowledge shared between the many individual minds that made up the whole. And when the afternoon sun caught on the underside of each wing in sequence, graduating the progression of light over the whole fluid structure as it turned with perfect elegance through a whole series of angles and relationships, something – just a feeling – kicked deep in my stomach and shot upwards, catching in my chest with a gratifying kind of pain. It made me stop walking and stare at the birds.

And it felt as though all the many versions of myself I'd dispersed around the city – attached to different jobs and people and scattered around various different news channels and live feeds – versions of myself that I'd dispersed around the whole world, even, in all the past events I'd somewhere logged as significant, and in all the futures that I knew more parts of myself than I was aware of must be obsessively planning – it was as if all of these scattered elements had touched down together in that field. As if they were all, for a moment, looking out of the same eyes – *my* eyes, I could finally confidently say. I felt inexpressibly grateful and just . . . relieved. And exhausted.

And so we stood still and watched, the many divisions of myself and I – we watched as these birds held themselves together with the kind of impossible magnetism I hadn't even managed to muster in the government of my own soul. It was a kind of master code being demonstrated in the sky, each bird shining in such beautiful context, yet still so utterly, evidently, recklessly free.

I stood and watched until the feeling subsided. Really this only took a couple of minutes but I suppose I tried to artificially suspend the revelation and stayed there until I was cold.

As I walked down the hill I took out my phone to call Annalise. She would appreciate my realisation, I thought. I listened to the phone ringing and I wondered – what was it exactly that I had experienced? And how would I explain it to her so that she understood? Should I tell her that I had seen a beautiful formation of birds in the sky and under-stood the harmony of the universe? No. Because that was trite and a vast simplification of the reality. What then?

Her phone stopped ringing and clicked through to voicemail. What was she doing ignoring her phone? Anna-lise never missed my calls. I dialled again. More ringing.

The birds couldn't just be birds. Or why would I have felt so . . . *moved* by them? They had to signify something bigger, something more universal. But I couldn't get back the feeling, couldn't recall it strongly enough to explain it or to rationalise it, even to myself. I may have witnessed something extraordinary but now I was just a man on a phone walking quickly down a hill trying to raise his body temperature and reach the train station before dark.

The phone was still ringing in my ear. I judged that I had just a few seconds to decide what to say to her. Well then I thought I'd tell her . . . that I'd stood on a hill in Somerset and discovered that revelation is real and that while life may be filled with disappointment and terror harmony does manifest fleetingly in moments of clarity so sharp that if you snatch at them each one brings with it an instant of something like redemption. Yes, Annalise would appreciate that. But why was she still not answering? I switched the phone on to speakerphone and checked the headlines again as I waited, crossing into the next field and listening as her phone continued to ring.

The Flat Roof

The Flat Roof

Annie's new flat had a flat roof. She could crawl out of the window of the upstairs landing and sit on top of the concrete monolith she called home, letting the world go by. She liked the way the sounds of distant clocks reached her up there, probably from way across the city. And some-times, she could hear her neighbours arguing, shouting to each other in the courtyards below.

She sang, often, up there, or she picked out chords on Tom's guitar and hummed the melodies of songs he used to sing. She tried to write things down too, carefully selecting the words she would use to try to capture how it felt to have lost him in this way – that, or she scribbled letters to her parents, apologising, explaining what had happened, and asking if they'd like to see her again, maybe, sometime, now that he was gone. She never sent any of them, those letters. She merely folded them up into paper planes and flew them off the roof into the sky, where they fluttered on the wind like leaves, or soared like the birds that circled round her there, as she watched the city's rooftops.

Seagulls wheeled and screeched, fighting for perches and food; pigeons bobbed and fluttered, looking so battered and threadbare here, in the city, compared to how they were at home. Crows paced up and down, tapping the concrete with harsh talons and beaks, and looking fiercer and more unforgiving than Annie was quite comfortable with. Smaller songbirds – blackbirds, starlings, finches, sparrows – would flutter on and off the low rail that lined the very edge of the roof on all sides, adding their voices to Annie's quiet, whispery singing as she watched their wings, and tried to hear the ghostly voice behind her own as she lost herself in those familiar tunes.

Annie probably spent too much time on her flat roof. But these days, without Tom, still with no job here in the city, and feeling ever more strongly that she needed just a little longer before she tried to look for one, she really didn't have anywhere else she needed to be. It seemed as good a place as any to sit quietly, passing the hours, waiting to feel ready to face the world again.

She waited all through February, shivering, wrapped in Tom's coat and layers and layers of scarves. She waited through March as the new leaves appeared and filled out the canopy of trees extending beyond the city's rooftops – and then into April, when the first swallows began to arrive, diving and dipping their wings.

Still with the coat round her shoulders, but losing some of the scarves now, she felt the roof become a much less punishing place to be – much warmer, both literally and in terms of atmosphere. For it was around this time she started noticing a change, she was sure, in the behaviour of the birds. When she'd first moved in, they would rarely land while she was sitting there, only wheel around, squawking and gasping as if affronted at the violation of their territory. Now, though, they seemed to be getting used to her, and were pecking and fluttering wherever they pleased. At first, just for a day or two, Annie felt it wasn't fair that she should be overlooked like this, as she had just as much right to be part of life on the roof as they did. Then, though, she realised it wasn't quite that they were ignoring her. It was, rather, that in the days and weeks since she'd arrived they'd grown used to her, so that now they counted her almost as one of their own.

Once she'd figured this out it became quite fun to sit on her chair and observe them interacting around her, fighting and flirting and stealing. She even branched out from singing those old songs of Tom's and began to make up simple melodies all of her own, which expressed, she hoped, something of what it felt to be amongst the birds like this, watching the patterns of the swallows and swifts as they swept their wild ways through the sky. She scattered crumbs of stale bread around her feet, and even lifted up handfuls to the poor, worn-out pigeons, who would land on her hands and her arms and her shoulders, finding nourishment and rest, at last, in this little thing that she could offer them.

April wore on into May, the sun burnt hot above her, and even though Annie needed sunscreen now to stop her skin from burning, she still wore Tom's coat. After all, it wasn't quite summer yet, and sometimes in the evenings it could still get quite cold. And then, of course, the talons of the birds would feel so harsh if they landed on her without the coat's protection – and also . . . well. In spite of it being months, now, since he'd last worn it, she was sure that it still smelt of him, a little.

As she grew to know it better, life among the birds became quite exciting. One early afternoon in June, for instance, a seagull landed bearing a chicken leg in its beak, pursued by a whole train of rivals. They fought it out on the roof, shrieking and circling and ripping bits of flesh off the bone and clawing at each other if a competitor got too close. A whole fleet of little pigeons descended too, then, to provide a kind of audience – gathering around Annie's feet as she sat in her chair and nodding their fat little heads in excitement, commenting to each other and hoping, perhaps, for some of the leavings if the seagulls got bored of the bone before it was picked clean. Annie felt her face crack into a grin for the first time in weeks – months, almost half a year – as she forgot herself a moment and joined in with all of them, just another spectator to the fight, gleefully shouting encouragements and warnings to her favourite seagulls, and flapping her hands about when things got too violent.

Only sometimes, now, did Annie feel out of sorts: when, nestled in her coat, happily surrounded by her new friends, they would suddenly take off all at once, as if all of one mind. She could never detect the signals that triggered one of these mass exits, and even if she had been able to, she didn't know what she'd have been able to do about it. She could hardly join in, after all. But still, she'd have liked a little more warning. It would have only been polite. Or she would have preferred if they didn't do it when she was in the middle of sentences, at least. She supposed, though, that this was simply how things were done here in the city. People had warned her about it, after all. They'd said it was the kind of place where people could just disappear.

When the birds left her in this way she would always jump up from her chair (a fraction later than the rest of them; a silly, insecure part of her hoped that they didn't notice this) and run with them as far as the roof's edge. There she would stand, hands on the rail, following the fleet into the sky with her eyes and leaning forward as far as she could, dazzled by sunlight. They were birds, she had to remind herself, and it was in their nature to need to fly away sometimes. Just as she was a woman, and it was in her nature to stay with her feet on the ground – even if that ground was sixty feet above a city, on a concrete platform in the sky. So she didn't feel left behind, really, when they flew. Or not for long, anyway, because they always came back.

Until one day, they didn't. It was a Thursday, and when Annie climbed out on to the roof that morning it was strangely empty of birds. Not in the way it had been at the beginning, when she'd first moved in and they'd all been sizing her up, wheeling around the edges, figuring out whether she was to be trusted or not. That day there were no birds at all. Or at least, there were some, of course, soaring in skeins in the distance, silhouetted against the bright sky. But none so near that Annie could see their faces, or their eyes, or the individual feathers that made up their wings.

She waited all morning for her friends to return. And when they didn't, she crawled back through the window and went to her kitchen to make a cheese sandwich. She ate quickly, standing up, and then clambered back on to the roof again, pulling the coat tighter around her and repositioning her chair slightly, moving it out of the heat of the afternoon sun.

She found she didn't know what to do without the birds there. All her favourite daily activities had built themselves around them. She couldn't sing to them or make up new songs without any of them near her. And anyway, recently she hadn't been doing so much of that. It did make her feel a little guilty, but Tom's old guitar had spent most of the last few weeks propped up against the wall by her window, next to the satellite dishes, while she'd spent most of that time simply talking, making better friends with certain individuals among the birds. She loved listening to the strange sounds and pitches their voices made. She loved the way they clicked their beaks, and how they gestured, mid-speech, with little distinctive twitches of their necks.

She'd told her new friends everything. It had been so nice, such a relief to finally say it all out loud instead of simply writing letter after unsent letter to her parents. And how wonderful it was to explain it to people who were kind, who cared about her, even, and who had never met Tom either, and so received everything she said about him with the same kindness, and the same understanding warmth. She didn't only talk about him, though – or about the nameless child they'd lost – she told the birds about happier, quieter days too. About the town she came from in the west, where everything was built from golden stone, bricks that glowed every time the sun came out, just as if fires had been lit somewhere deep inside them. She told them about the guinea pigs she'd had when she was small, and the hillside near their house, with the view over the train station, where her mum and dad had taken her for picnics every summer. And she told them, too, about how grateful and lucky she felt to have been able to find a place for herself here in the city, a new life with such wonderful friends, when even a few months ago she'd have thought such a thing impossible – unimaginable, even. She told them she'd never felt so safe and so looked after as she did on this roof, especially in the fading light of summer evenings, surrounded by their friendly feathered faces. They'd nodded at that, and many eyes had smiled appreciation.

Now suddenly she was alone. She knew it was silly to worry, and that they'd probably be back tomorrow, full of stories of some adventure. She only wished they'd told her about it beforehand. It would have been nice to sit here on this day alone, thinking of what they might all be getting up to in far-off places. But she didn't mind. She reminded herself again that it was only in their nature to need to fly away once in a while, just as it was in hers to stay grounded. She wished she'd taken a few pictures of herself with them, though. Just in case.

She waited there in her chair until nightfall, nestling deeper into the folds of the coat, not even leaving the roof to get a hot drink or a blanket when the temperature dropped. She didn't want any of them to think she'd forgotten them, if they did come back.

It wasn't until about half-past eleven that anything happened. When the city was as dark as the city would ever

get, and the stars had come out, glittering in patterned constellations, overlaid as usual with the crisscrossing lights of
distant planes.

It started with her noticing an aberration on the
horizon: a patch of sky darker than the rest of the vast,
sparkling sphere around her. An absence of light. A lack of
stars. She noticed it getting bigger. And bigger, and bigger.

Until it was vast and sweeping towards her like a fast,
softly rustling cloud. This was a bird on a different scale,
filling half the sky – a two-winged beast – a skein larger
than any Annie had ever seen before, soaring over the city,
right towards her roof.

Until it was so close that she could make out feathers,
eyes, and faces . . . and she cried out with sudden joy,
then, as she recognised at the head of the sky-fleet the most
beloved of her new friends, the ones whom she'd been sure
had nodded most gravely when she'd told them how happy
she was in her new life, here in the city with them. Her eyes
widened then, though, to see that behind these known and
dear and dearly missed friends were hundreds upon hundreds of faces, eyes and feathers that she didn't recognise;
that didn't look familiar to the city at all, for that matter.
Types of birds she'd only ever heard about before, with
wider wings, brighter plumages, sharper talons and new,
unfamiliar calls.

Annie had abandoned her chair long ago and was

standing now as she always did at the times when the birds suddenly left her: two hands on the rail, gazing out. She wondered how long they'd been flying today. How far they'd come and over what lands they'd soared whilst she'd made her cheese sandwich and sat in her chair.

But the pang of sadness that passed through her as she thought about this was left largely unacknowledged, because when this vast night bird descended on her roof, she felt instead the sharp scratchings of a hundred small talons as they gripped her fingers, raked her hair, jabbed through the material of Tom's coat, and even hooked themselves around her wrists and arms and ankles.

She felt a flash of fear then, and a part of her wondered about struggling, fighting off whatever was happening and running back to shelter inside. It was, for a moment, as if she were a woman afraid of drowning, unwilling to breathe out and embrace the flood of water around her.

Then, though, eyes wild, searching for the escape route of her open window, her gaze found Tom's guitar, still propped against the bricks – and all of her uncertainty vanished, washed away in the tides of grief and hope that finally coursed through her, unabated. She opened her arms wide to the birds, letting more of them flutter down until almost every inch of her skin and of his old coat was covered with their folded feathers.

Then, as one, they beat their wings. And with a gentleness that could have broken Annie's heart all over again, they lifted her – first up on to her tiptoes, and then until she was hovering, flying, suspended inches from the ground.

She let out a cry, so wild and so avian that she would surely have surprised herself had she not been too overcome to be listening, and her bird-friends answered it, a unified call echoing back to her from all the many faces and voices. She wondered whether she was going mad, or if she really could feel strange muscles and virgin feathers emerging from her shoulder blades.

She grasped the rail, then, and lifted herself up so that she was standing on it, poised and balanced, still held up by the birds. And as she stepped off the roof, falling into clear, open space, she spread her arms like wings, stretching out her fingers.

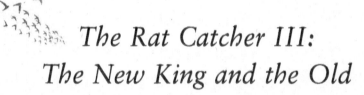

The Rat Catcher III:
The New King and the Old

My mother died when I was very young. She exists as not much more to me than fragments of remembered warmth, of brightness and laughter in the palace, and snatches of the lullabies she used to sing to me before I slept.

It was only recently, when I was travelling in the eastern territories, that word came of my father's death. It was the first time in all my life I'd been away from the palace for an extended interval of time, and losing my last remaining parent in this way felt like some awful reproach for leaving his side. It was as if something almost supernatural was at work, punishing me for my absence. The timing of the whole thing was, I felt sure, simply too neat for a coincidence.

I can't remember much from those weeks after my return – everything seemed to move so quickly. My very first night back, though, stays vivid: letting myself in through the front door, using my own keys instead of knocking, hoping not to wake anyone so that I might spend a few hours at least in peace. I crossed the hall, creeping in stockinged feet, and went up the central stairs to the first floor, where I let myself into a little parlour leading off from the main corridor.

I had just set my case down when the door behind me creaked open, making me start round guiltily, expecting to see the old housekeeper, or my sister, or more likely one of her monstrous rodent friends come to sniff me out now I'd returned. And yet I was surprised by a very strange event – by a magical one, almost – for it was not a rat there in the doorway at all, but a small dog with a funny, crinkled face that somehow made me want to laugh. What an unexpected thing it was to happen. Quite as if the little creature had known he'd find me there, or even as if he'd been sent by some mysterious, powerful force, expressly to welcome me home.

'Hello, friend,' I greeted him, crouching down to rub his furry coat. 'Did someone send you here? Did someone send you to look after me?'

I put my hand out for him to sniff and he nuzzled into it, all kindness, warmth and trust.

'You'd suit being called Lucas,' I told him, and he spent the night curled on the rug in front of the fire while I settled in the armchair, my coat pulled over me in place of a blanket. As the wind tore through the rest of the house I remember feeling almost happy for a moment, imagining the two of us as stowaways on a vast ghost ship, keeping warm together as we sheltered from the storm.

My memories grow blurred again when I consider all the days that follow. The only other episode that exists with any clarity begins with my taking Lucas in my arms, and making my way up the stairs to my father's apartments. We met no human beings at all as we wandered through the corridors and halls, only rats. And I remember thinking it odd, for though life at the palace had certainly been much reduced since my early childhood, when Mother was still living and people were always about, it didn't feel right for it to be quite so very deserted as that.

'Do you feel it, little Luke?' I remember saying. 'I wonder what can be wrong.'

I tried the handles of a few locked doors near to where my father had his office, and was close to giving up and taking us off in search of the warmth of a fireplace again when a door I had my hand on clicked open almost magically, so smoothly that it was as if the mechanism had just been oiled.

We stepped inside, little Luke and I, to see my father laid out on a grand four-poster bed, perfectly preserved and dressed in the kind of clothing he might have worn for giving a state address. Luke started barking and whining in fear, or perhaps simply at the thick smell in the room: something foul overlaid with a powerful mix of cleaning chemicals, and the sweet, floral scent of the candles that burnt on every surface. He looked so much older than I'd expected, somehow, my father. So wasted and thin, utterly depleted like that, with no spirit left to fill his body. I turned to leave, to take myself as far away as I could manage, but there was a man standing there, in the doorway. I hadn't heard the slightest hint of his approach. He extended his hand for me to shake.

'My name is Shaw,' he said. 'Your sister summoned me to oversee proceedings concerning the matter of your father's will. It seems, I am afraid, that not everything was left so clear as you might wish.'

'My sister?' I remember saying to him. 'But she had no right. My father hated her.' But the man simply stared at me as Luke growled and snapped around his ankles . . .

Then there was the coronation. That strange day of cheering citizens, rodents skipping everywhere, and me in the middle of it all, standing uncomfortable in formal dress at the top of a tall flight of steps. I spotted my sister in the crowd, and she smiled at me and still looked furious. I wished then – wished with all my heart – that everyone would go away and I could be alone with only little Luke for company, somewhere far from my father's body and from my sister and her rodent friends, and that nasty lawyer Shaw.

Indeed, it did occur to me that there was a cottage in the woods, was there not? Some groundsman's house from long ago? I found myself resolving, as I stood there, still bowing and waving to the citizens, that as soon as that miserable coronation was over I would leave the palace, taking with me only Luke and some provisions from the kitchens, and I would disappear, never to return to its nightmarish halls again.

*

Yet not even a single month has passed since I made my resolution, and here I am, back in my father's room, sitting at his bedside! The candles and the incense are still burning, and his dear old body is laid out just as it was before – reeking, I am now sure, of what must be formaldehyde. I try my best, though, to ignore that nasty, clinical scent of his, and I reach for his mottled hand – because I came here, you understand, in the shadow of the burning man, and desperate for advice.

I concentrate as hard as I am able, doing my best to think of what my father might say to me if he were still living, if he were simply sick, perhaps, and I were here as his dutiful son, come to visit him. And yet I find that nothing comes to me, and I cannot reassure myself with any recollected friendly words of his at all. The quiet of the room begins to grate on my already fragile nerves, and in the end I break the silence first.

'Father, I'm sorry,' I say. 'I've done what I think might

be a terrible thing. I'm rather afraid I've let you down already.'

My father persists in remaining quite still and quite silent.

'But what should I do now?' I ask, trying to keep myself from clutching at his fragile hand too roughly. 'Do tell me, Father, please. I never intended to hurt anybody, truly. It was an accident, almost. Quite simply the result of a moment's being carried away.'

I wait for words to come, some piece of advice or reassurance he might offer to shed a less fearful light on what occurred that awful morning in the forest, when I seized the top beam of the burning man's machine – horrible to think that he was not yet burning then – and dragged it through the fire. I wait and wait by my father's side until I find I cannot bear the silence of his room any longer, and then I run back out of the palace and into the trees, where every flutter in the canopy sounds to me like the wings of angels, sent down from heaven to deliver my judgement. Oh, I am a monster, that much is very clear. It is no wonder he refuses to talk with me.

*

It is night-time now and, even though I'm sure that Luke is angry with me, I return to the cabin to check on him. It is essential, you understand, for me to keep a close watch on him, seeing as he is now so sick and weak and sad.

It does occur to me as I see him there, curled up in our usual corner, nestled in the blankets with his tiny chin resting on his front paws, gazing unblinkingly with melancholy eyes, that probably he would appreciate some diversion or entertainment to while away the dark hours until it's time for us to sleep and dream again. And yet I am too far from my usual self to think of any game that might be fun for him. I am still too shaken even to think of gathering him into my arms and comforting him that way. We have both, you see, been quite transformed by what occurred and are not ourselves at all. Luke does not complain, though, at my neglect. His silent looks seem only to reproach me very gently for my cowardice as I sit across the floor from him.

'Lucas,' I say, rubbing my hands for warmth – and I am afraid he must be cold, too, for I am certainly too cautious to light the fire these days – 'do you ever wonder if things really happened as you think they did?'

I raise a hand to rub my eyes and, as I do, I'm certain I glimpse him twitch an ear in my direction.

'Oh, Luke,' I continue, edging closer towards him on the floor. 'Truly, I am quite afraid, for I am beginning to doubt the reliability of my memory. It's as if so many wild, unlikely things have happened recently that my poor, sad brain cannot quite make sense of all of them, and sort the true from the imagined. I have been trying, for instance, to remember all the things that happened in the days after I arrived back at the palace, and yet I find my recollections from that time – only several weeks ago – to be quite disordered and unclear. And then my father, Luke. This puzzles me, too. Because as I remember it, my father wasn't . . .' But as Luke gazes at me, waiting, no doubt, for me to give some satisfactory explanation for my cold, distant behaviour, I feel my eyes begin to run, and I have to break off a moment to wipe them on my sleeve. 'I don't remember him being so cruel a man as to leave me without any guidance, or advice,' I carry on, when I find myself able to speak clearly again. 'To leave me alone in this kingdom of vipers, with nothing at all that might help.'

Little Luke, though, offers no gesture of understanding or forgiveness, and as is so usual for me in these days I am left to feel disconsolate, ready to weep until I fall into a sickness, and from there into more troubled dreams . . . Except that suddenly, tonight, I am distracted by a voice from by the door.

'If you'll excuse me, Your Majesty,' it says, in haughty tones – for it is Shaw, you see, that smug, deceiving creature, standing framed in my cabin's entrance, blocking out the moonlight – 'I couldn't help but notice you neglected to collect your bread and water from the kitchens.'

He's right, of course. I haven't felt like eating since our morning with the burning man, but I had not even considered that this might provide him with yet another excuse to come and call on me here, to gloat and posture in this way, at little Luke and me.

'I took the liberty – I hope you'll forgive me – of bringing some provisions for you, as I was taking my evening constitutional.' At that, Shaw draws back a napkin to unveil a loaf of bread and a can of water cradled in the crook of his arm – identical in all appearances to those that I had indeed fallen into the habit of taking from the kitchens every week or so – more for Lucas' sustenance than for my own, you understand, for ever since my infancy it seems I have been able to survive on very little. All instincts, then, tell me to refuse this offer of Shaw's and to turn him forthwith from my door, but my little Lucas must be starving.

'I thank you, Shaw,' I say. 'If you'll just leave them –' I gesture with a filthy, tear-stained hand to the corner of the cabin furthest from me – 'over there, that'll do quite nicely.'

'Of course, Your Majesty,' says Shaw, depositing the bread and water without taking his eyes off me. 'If you'll beg pardon, Your Majesty,' he carries on, 'and you won't mind my saying it . . .'

'Out with it, Shaw, I'm busy.'

'Is Your Majesty lacking a razor and some soap? If you would like – and only if this really would be your prefer-ence – I could bring you some examples of the same on my next trip down?'

'It is kind of you to suggest it,' I say, pronouncing each word carefully – and I notice that my voice does not sound quite like my own, and that perhaps, even, if someone were close by, they might remark that both my tone and manner of delivery bear indeed a close resemblance to my father's – 'and I thank you, Shaw, but I manage perfectly well out here without any help from you . . .' Then my eyes stray to Luke again, and suddenly my defiance is all drained away, and I only feel exhausted. 'Oh, but I have not the heart for any of your games tonight, Shaw. Do leave us alone now, please. My dog is not well.'

'Evidently, Your Majesty.'

'And I am not myself tonight.'

'If you say so, Majesty.'

The wind rattles the roof, birds shriek outside, and yet still he does not leave us.

'I am currently engaged in making arrangements for your father's burial,' he says at last, after a long interval of simply staring at me. 'I trust you'll adopt a more fitting demeanour in time for the funeral.'

264

I feel suddenly sick, and not a little faint. 'Burial, Shaw?' I find myself asking him. 'Is it not – does he really have to be – buried?'

'That is the standard procedure, Your Majesty.'

'I am well aware of that. But, my father.'

'Yes, Your Majesty?'

'Surely that stinking cell of a room you've got him shut up in now is prison enough?'

'Then you've been to visit him again,' he says.

'I have.'

'You must hardly recognise him.'

'I would always recognise my father, Shaw.'

He simply shrugs at that, and flicks a speck of dust from off his sleeve.

'Shaw?'

'Yes, Your Majesty?'

'Tell me again. What did he die of – my father?'

'Old age, Your Majesty.'

'Just old age, Shaw?'

'Precisely, Your Majesty.'

'And you are quite certain, Shaw – oh, but how shall I put this? – you are *quite sure*, that there was nothing perhaps *more specific*?'

'Not that I am aware of, Your Majesty. A precise cause of death is often too complex to pinpoint when the deceased in question is as frail as your father was.'

Shaw's lips curl themselves up until he's positively smiling, an expression I rarely witness on that ugly face of his, and not one that I appreciate being there at all.

*

After he finally leaves us there is nothing left for little Luke and me except to sit wrapped in our best blankets, staring at the dark, frost-covered walls. Even though I know very well that we are out in the forest, surrounded by trees and flying birds and open ground, something about that last visit seems to have stolen all the life from the air. As the minutes and then the hours tick by, I slowly come to realise that as much as I'd hate to leave Luke in the sad condition that he's in, vulnerable to any carrion crow or rodent who might find its way into our home without me there to defend it, I have another duty to fulfil up at the palace.

'I have to go away now for a while,' I tell Lucas. 'I must go to my father, before they put him in the ground.'

Luke gazes at me then – so small and noble and defenceless – and yet still I find I cannot bear to take him in my arms.

'I know, little Luke,' is all I can muster. 'I'm sorry. I know.'

*

'Father.' I am back inside his room, now, clinging to his hand. 'Father, I don't want you to be buried and trapped under layers of earth. What do you think, Father?'

I grip his hand ever tighter, and then realise with a jolt of alarm that I am harming it. Because, oh, it is a thing that is easy enough to do. It's a poor, old, fragile hand, after all, and the skin itself has no elasticity left, none at all, and now the whole construction, indeed, seems to stretch and warp within my grasp.

'Father, oh, I'm sorry!' I drop the hand and then reach out for it again, doing my best to rearrange it so that it rests quite properly back at his side, and I try – I do, I try my utmost – not to hurt him as I twist and crack his fingers back into position. 'You're tired,' I tell him. 'I shouldn't be putting this strain on you, Father. Perhaps I shouldn't have come to disturb you at all.'

I am just bending down to plant a kiss upon his papery, wrinkly forehead when a marvellous idea sparks in my mind.

It would be a risk, certainly, but surely one worth taking. And it might necessitate a small element of disruption, but nothing too unmanageable. After all, there isn't much left in this world I can still do for him, but surely I could manage this? Surely I could give my father one last night of freedom, out and about in the world in the company of his only and devoted son?

I decide upon it there and then. I shall take him out on an adventure, just the two of us, walking arm in arm. We shall match each other's stride, and he shall lean his weight upon me as he limps, and then he shall point out to me certain key features of interest that strike him as we move through the palace, bringing the cold rooms of our home back to life as we make our way through the halls. He will tell me the stories, for instance, depicted in the tapestries, and the meanings of the designs of the fireplaces, and then he shall talk all about the subjects of the paintings on the central stairway, leading up into the ballroom . . . and oh, we will explore and explore, seeing the whole palace with new eyes until at last we shall be so tired out with walking that he shall turn to me, my father, and ask if there isn't some place I can think of where we might sit awhile, and talk together, while we rest our poor aching feet. And then, of course, I shall lead him outside – outside! To the parks, to sit out upon the grass and under the trees, for how long must it have been since he last tasted clean air, shut up in this awful room as he is? And then when we are both out under the open sky, I shall sling one arm around his old shoulders and begin to show him the stars. *How perfect that would be*, I think to myself as I sit at his side. What a treat for us both. Why on earth has it never occurred to me to do such a thing before now?

And so, ever so carefully, I slide my hands and arms

around and under his torso – for a moment indeed it might look to anyone watching as though we were embracing – and like this I begin to manoeuvre him from the bed.

But he is heavier – far, far heavier – than I could have expected.

I imagined, I think, that I might cradle him in my arms like a child and carry him like that, and yet as it is, my technique for moving him adapts itself to his weight, until I must confess it comes to resemble something closer to a gentle kind of dragging. Inching us from the bed towards the door in minute degrees, I soothe him and utter reassuring words with every step, explaining to him that he can trust me, and that I will look after him, and yet it is awkward work indeed, to shift him so. His frame is rigid and difficult to manipulate, while the flesh itself feels loose upon the bones, and somewhat unstable. He could never have managed something so taxing as this on his own, I cannot help but think. He is lucky indeed to have such a daring and devoted son.

After what seems like hours we've made it to the door. I was planning to take him down the main staircase, so that we would be able to wander the halls, and then make our way out through the door by the kitchens, to view the stars from there, but it's become quite evident over just this short distance that I shall have to rethink my plan entirely to something less ambitious. Completely aside from the question of my own strength and ability to support him over such a distance, I see now that my father is far weaker than I thought, and I simply cannot be sure, you understand, that his body could bear such a difficult journey. And so I turn our steps away from the main part of the palace, making instead for the battlements.

'It's all right, Father, you can trust me. We're just going on a little trip – one last small excursion. Whatever Ethel and Shaw may say, you're not going into the ground quite yet!'

I imagine him nodding and chuckling at that, lit up with mischief at our unexpected adventure.

'That's the spirit,' I whisper to him. 'One last hurrah. Just the two of us.'

And, 'Just the two of us,' I repeat back to myself in reply, in my best effort at a gentle, elderly voice to match his kindly wrinkles.

His feet drag loudly on the floor as we go and I cannot help but begin to suspect that it must be quite painful for him – this method of travelling – and that he is simply being stoic in not complaining or even mentioning it. Out of fear, perhaps, of hurting my feelings.

'Oh, Father,' I breathe as soon as I realise it, and I kneel down to manoeuvre myself so that I'm crouched alongside his body, where I can lift him by his rigid legs with one hand, and support him under his torso with the other. And

I discover that, like this, if I keep shuffling my crouching position sideways in our direction of travel, he can move down the length of the corridor quite nicely, rather in the manner of a man swimming through air.

And so we are going on fairly well, my father and I, when all at once I hear a rustling of material behind me. I twist my head round to discover what the cause of it might be – my fear, you understand, is that it is one of the palace's rodents, come to investigate the scent – and yet I soon see that it is, perhaps, something rather worse. For there is my sister, standing in a doorway behind me, her expression arranged in such a way as to suggest a kind of trepidation, even horror. Our eyes meet and, purely on instinct, I find myself hunching forward, bending further over my father – quite ready, indeed, to protect him if need be. For once, though, Ethel seems to be mostly benign, simply rooted to the spot, and silent. *Good*, I think, as I study her there in her apparent surprise. Perhaps in seeing me and our father side by side like this – in having such an opportunity, that is, to observe the bond between us at close quarters – she will grow quite ashamed of herself, and of the way she has treated us. I narrow my eyes at her and continue with our slow shuffle onwards, thinking she'll go away now and leave us in peace. And yet still she watches, seemingly transfixed, until a bend in the corridor hides her from our sight.

'Don't worry, Father, she shan't bother us again,' I say, trying to reassure him, sounding more brisk, perhaps, than I really feel. 'She's nobody, after all, no one at all. She doesn't mean any harm.'

Oh, but the false reassurance sticks in my throat, and I have to remind myself I am telling this untruth with the best of intentions, hoping only that my father might breathe a little more easily believing nothing is amiss, despite the unplanned nature of the encounter. It is an important thing, I think, that tonight of all nights, on this final trip of ours, he feels he can trust his only son to take good care of him.

At last we reach the small wooden door I've been piloting us towards – the door to the spiralling steps leading up to the battlements – and I find I have to lay him down for a moment on the icy floor while I fumble with the latch. And oh, how sorry I am for that. His skin already feels so terribly cold.

And then to make matters worse, once I've got the door open, lifting him again proves such difficult work. My muscles don't seem to want to return to bearing such a heavy load so promptly after all that exertion. And yet they must – now that we have come so far – and I tell them so, hoisting him back up into my arms with, I hope, only a minimum of jostling and bodily disruption. But what, I wonder, can be the best way of getting him up the stairs?

I begin trying several different methods, but each quickly proves to be hopeless and impracticable, either too uncomfortable for me to sustain, or too likely to cause him pain, though he never utters a word of complaint.

In the end I find that if I sit on the steps with him below me, and hook my arms underneath his shoulders, I can shift myself backwards, up the staircase, pulling him along with me. It isn't ideal. His legs catch and clatter against the twisting stone with echoing reverberations, but he is a strong man, I know. And what adventure worth undertaking doesn't cause a few bruises along the way?

After what seems like an eternity of this shifting and banging we reach the top of the stairs. I push open the door and haul him up, and we both fall headlong on to the battlements, our limbs quite entangled, gasping for breath. Oh, how good it is to be out in the night – just the two of us, finally – breathing clear air.

*

I am the first to recover, being the younger man. And so I remove my jacket, fold it, and place it under my father's tired head. Then I do my best to arrange the rest of him so that he appears comfortable, dragging him a little further away from the door as I do so, in such a way that allows us to lie side by side and both of us have a clear view of the open sky, unimpeded by the shadow of the palace walls.

'Do you know, Father, the names of all the constellations?' I ask him, once we are finally settled. 'That one there is a good place to start.' I take hold of his arm with one hand and angle it so that it points up at the sky. 'The Plough,' I tell him, 'is probably the easiest of all of them to spot, but I don't think that makes it any less beautiful.' And I trace the sparks of light with my own fingertip for him to see, in case his old eyes are not so clear as once they were. 'And that one there,' I continue, 'that's Pegasus, the winged horse. And next to it is Andromeda, the chained maiden. Those aren't as clear to see at first, but you'll soon get good at spotting them, Father, I'm sure.'

I find myself yawning, and let my hand fall to my side. I suddenly feel so very tired, quite as if some great burden has been taken from me after some unknowably long time. And so I nestle my head into my father's shoulder, and let my eyes drift shut.

'A terrible thing happened the other day, Father,' I tell him. 'A sick and injured man with yellow teeth and such a funny accent came into my cabin, and Luke and I thought we might make some amusement out of him, but it was foolish of us, really. We should have let him alone; I see that now. Then maybe everything would still be quite all right.'

He is silent, as usual, but his silence has a potent quality to it now. As if he's listening hard, weighing up what I'm telling him.

And it is such a relief to finally be speaking to him in this frank and easy manner that I let myself continue talking as drowsiness envelops me ever more deeply in its folds.

'I never wanted to tell you this before, Father,' I say then, 'though now I can't think why, quite, but you see . . . I'm not sure if I like the idea of being king, after all. Not only for myself, you understand. I cannot help but wonder – cannot help but feel – that surely . . . is it not simply too much responsibility for just one man to have?'

The wind blows soft around us, lifting my hair and soothing my forehead. And from the comfort of the dark behind my closed eyelids the night seems to spin and weave itself around us like a cloak, and an old lullaby wanders into my mind. I begin to hum it to him as we drift, until . . .

'My son,' my father says – and not in the benign, elderly voice I conjured for him at all, but in harsh tones, which now I hear them again are familiar as anything – and suddenly I am transformed once more into a hapless child, sent to see him in his study, squinting up into his disappointed face. 'My son,' he says to me, 'you have lost your way.'

I lurch from him so wildly I collide with the outer wall of the battlements. Surely I would have tumbled off and out into the night had that wall been lower. Then I'm scrambling away from him as fast as I am able, and my eyes don't see the stars any more but a dark and dizzy mess of flagstones as I crawl back to the door, taking myself away, swiftly out of his sight. And yet his voice rings out again to pincer me with its derision.

'Call yourself a son of mine?' it says. 'Tell me, how could such an exalted line as ours have ended in such uselessness, in such pathetic lack of judgement? Even your wicked sister would make a better king than you.'

I scramble to my feet and run the final stretch over the flagstones to the door, then stumble down the spiral staircase, crashing into walls and slipping down whole sets of steps at once on my flailing heels, feeling the shock of impact in my bones. And then I'm flying along the corridor, down the main staircase, past the old housekeeper – she swivels her head short-sightedly at me as I go – through the green baize door, past the kitchens, until finally I'm clattering my way out of the back entrance and sprinting the stretch of snowy ground to the trees, which tonight are filled with black wings, with birds screaming, and with shadows flickering.

*

At last the sky above the treetops begins to brighten, and some of the horror subsides. I sit down to rest in the snow, only to discover that I am, in fact, quite unsure of where in the forest I might be, even though I did think I knew these woodlands as well as the lines on my own palms. How on earth can it be that I still haven't found my way home? And where, indeed, is the palace in relation to where I am now? It is impossible, after all, to lose sight of that from anywhere in the parks. It is ever-present here. Quite impossible to lose.

I look about myself more calmly and find it easily enough, its façade gleaming above the canopy in the first flickers of the dawn, crows circling it, like always. I feel so much better after having got my bearings, and with the reassurance of some sunlight, that I forget myself a moment, and consider going home. I imagine I will light a fire and snuggle up before it with my little Luke, so that we both might pass the day in getting warm. Then in the evening there might be games for us to play, unless of course we feel quite tired, in which case we could simply rest and go on with our jigsaw puzzle. It's only as my eyes fix on the birds, soaring round and round the battlements, that my mind begins to clear, and I remember that there is no warm and cosy home for me to go to any more, for the burning man ruined all of that, and little Luke is gone.

The realisation brings hot tears into my eyes, and I am ready to give up, to lie down in the snow and weep, when I begin to recall something else. Was there not another thing I had to do? Something pressing and important? Something concerning, perhaps, the wellbeing of my father? And I begin to remember how I left him: up on the battlements, alone in the cold, fragile and frail, with not so much as a blanket for shelter. And then there are those dark birds, circling.

I leap straight to my feet and chase my way through the trees once again, weaving the most direct route I can manage back to my father, the pale warmth of the morning sun at my back as I scramble on, crows flying alongside me and calling to each other like heralds announcing my return. At last I'm running through the halls, and then taking those spiralling steps two at a time, all the way up to the battlements.

'Father, Father,' I call as I go. 'It's all right now, Father. I haven't forgotten you, Father!'

But as I tumble out into the dawn I find a savage process already underway. It isn't the crows – those creatures of judgement that, since the morning with the burning man, I've been so afraid might swoop down on poor depleted Luke – this is something else entirely, which, now I see it, makes an awful kind of sense. Because it's rats, of course. Rats, crawling all over my father, and of so monstrous a size that even I, who have spent so many years within the infested confines of the palace, find myself quite stunned. Their enormity seems significant, indeed – almost *deliberate* – as if they spent all those years feeding themselves on my sister's lonely offerings, breeding and gnawing and making themselves strong just so they might come prepared to this very occasion. There even seems to be a certain system in place amongst them, to allow for the fact that there is only room for a limited number of them on my father at any given time. Those of them with space and purchase on his body, that is, seem to remain in position for only as long as is required for them to scramble over each other's sinewy, shining backs to tear a portion of his flesh. Then this whole crowd of creatures departs for some quieter spot – by the high wall, perhaps, skirting the battlements – where they sit up on their haunches and peel back the skin of their mouths from their teeth and devour their takings, all while a new tide of rodents falls on him. *How efficient*, is all I am able to think. *How very, very efficient.*

I take a few careful steps towards my father, trying my best to shoo away some of the beasts, but they pay me no attention. And so I find myself falling to my knees, putting up my arms to shield my face, and venturing in amongst those rats myself, crawling and feeling my way, vying with them to lay my hands on him and salvage something that might count for my own share. And so the creatures crawl over me, too, the mass of them warm and heavy on my back and legs and arms and scalp, their feet sharp as they scramble for purchase. Then one of them is sinking its teeth into the heel of my hand – perhaps mistaking my flesh for my father's – and I fling my arm up, towards the sky, thinking to shake the beast loose. Somehow, though, it maintains its hold, even twists itself around so that its paws, too, are gripping me. *If only he had curbed them earlier on*, I find myself thinking. If only he had behaved differently to my sister, made some effort to find her fitting companions instead of raising her as if she were hardly better than vermin herself. If only he had loved her more, even, I wouldn't care. I wouldn't care at all, now, if he'd loved her more than he'd loved me, if only he'd done something – anything at all – that might have prevented her from nurturing these monsters; that might have given me some chance against them now.

The air is splintered, then, by the piercing sound of a whistle, and I look up from the tearing, chewing mass of bodies to see two familiar eyes watching me from the darkness of the nearest tower, glowing like coals in the night. *It's impossible*, is my first thought. I must have gone mad, or else this truly is a ghost, come to haunt me for my cruelty. For how can he still be living, after what I did to him? When I saw him run out into the trees like a comet, flames blazing over every inch of him?

Yet somehow, seemingly as real as anything, he steps out of the tower and into the dawn light of the roof. And as he does so I see with a jolt that under the coat he wears his skin is a strange, leathery mass of welts and puckers, of peeling shifting layers like the outside of an onion, and blackened patches and marks and bubbling, blistering wounds. For a moment I cannot help but think I must not be staring at a man at all, but at something like the surface of the sun.

'Your Majesty,' he says. And he nods his disfigured, completely hairless head, looking down on me, and on the rats, with an expression I cannot possibly read.

Then a rodent sinks its fangs into my ankle, and the pain jolts me from my horror and reminds me of the task at hand: pulling those awful creatures off my father.

'Your Majesty,' repeats the rat catcher – louder, this time – but I am caught up in tugging at the rats, prising one from what must once have been the flesh of my father's stomach, and finally shaking that most persistent one from my hand.

I hear him whistle again: a single, harsh note at first that then develops into a tune. He starts upon it quietly, but soon the sound begins to ring out louder, until it resembles no man's whistling I've ever heard before. It's a rough sound – not beautiful, exactly – but it carries through the dawn air like the call of a bird. And then, oh, then it is like some species of miracle. The rats around me stop with their tearing and scratching and fighting, and I watch as their ears spark up at the sound, and they sniff the air, and flick their tails. Finally they take their last mouthfuls of my poor, dear father's flesh and melt away, back into the cracks and holes in the walls and stone around us.

I sit up where I am and catch my breath a moment, staring out into the illuminated sky. Then I make myself look back down at my father's face, only to see that he's not there at all. There's nothing left of him other than white bone and ribbons of old flesh.

'If you would like to do the honours,' the rat catcher says, and I look up to see him holding something out to me in his hand. I flinch away from it at first, certain it must be some weapon, some threat, for surely that must be what he's here to do, to get his revenge, when I mutilated him so badly?

But looking down into the rat catcher's blistered, melted palm, I am surprised to see nothing more than a simple box of matches. What can he mean by showing them to me? I wonder if perhaps he means to set me alight, just as I did him.

'For your father, Majesty,' he says, at last. 'The cleanest way. I can't keep the rodents back for long.'

At last I understand what he means for me to do. I begin to tell him that I can't – that Shaw has other plans, and anyway my nerves are shot – but then I stop and really look at him, this damaged creature, almost unrecognisable as the man who came for me all those days ago through the trees, in the dark, so intent on destroying the one bright spot of comfort I'd managed to find in this world of sadness.

I reach out for the box of matches, trying not to flinch as my fingertips brush against his skin. My hands are shaking so badly it takes me three attempts to light one. He watches me steadily throughout as if overseeing the task, making certain it's done well. At last a match takes, and with a hasty, muttered prayer – *Dear Lord, please protect his soul* – I drop it, flaring, on my father's corpse. The flame sputters, fades, seems about to expire, until it catches on a piece of torn material that might once have been a shirt. It spreads quickly then – surprisingly so. The chemicals Shaw treated his body with must have altered his physical chemistry somehow, made him more susceptible to burning. I try to give the box of matches back to the rat catcher, but he sinks his hands into his pockets, and shakes his head.

And so I'm left to scrape another match across the box until it lights, and then to drop it down next to the line of flames that is already dancing over the full length of the ruined carcass.

And then I hear hurried footsteps coming up behind me, and a harsh little cry that jars me out of the almost trancelike state I have found, watching the flames take over the body. I turn to see Ethel rushing towards us over the battlements, with Shaw lagging behind. For once, though, my sister and her lawyer do not seem to be quite in accord, for Ethel appears to be in something of a state of shock. Reaching us, she hardly spares a glance for me – still holding the incriminating box of matches – or, for that matter, for the rat catcher, so hideously transformed. Instead, with apparently no thought to the state of her dress as it pools over the sooty, greasy flagstones, she sinks to her knees, staring fixedly into the flames.

Shaw finally arrives behind her. 'I suppose we'd better send for someone,' he says, after taking a short moment to look over the scene, 'to get all this cleared up.'

All this. He speaks as if it were some minor breakage – some teacup-sized disorder that could be swept up in a twinkling – and I am about to tell him exactly what I think of his treating this grave occasion with such flippancy when my sister stirs from her seeming reverie.

She doesn't lift her eyes from our father's burning husk, but she does open her painted lips, and say, 'That's enough, Shaw. I've had enough of you now. Please leave.'

For a moment he looks surprised, almost hurt. Then he shrugs and takes a few steps back from us along the parapet, settling down to sit upon a stone wall, and reach into his pocket for a cigarette.

No one else seems to want to speak, after that. We watch the body burn, and I find my eyes and throat stinging with the acrid quality of the smoke. I wonder how the rat catcher can bear it.

At a certain point, when no vestiges of human form are discernible within the fire and the smoke seems dense as tar, the crone appears, quietly taking her place amongst us. She, too, watches the burning for a moment, then she shakes her head, and disappears down the stairs into the palace. I don't much expect her to return, but it's not long before she's back, shuffling close up to the flames and reaching into the pockets of her dress, bringing out a stone, smooth and pale like the pebbles I saw on my travels, lining our country's eastern shore. Awkwardly, she manoeuvres herself into something of a crouch, and lays it on the ground close to the burning corpse. Then with almost excruciating slowness she straightens herself up, fumbles in her pocket for another, and squats down again, laying the second stone alongside the first. I stop wishing for her to speed up as she repeats the task again – building, I begin to see, a circle of these stones around the fire. There is a sense of ritual to her movements, and I discover that I find it almost comforting.

Not so, though, it seems, for my sister. All this time, both she and the rat catcher have been frozen as statues, each of them apparently lost to their own considerations as they watch the steady progress of the flames. But now something in her seems to crack.

'This isn't what I wanted at all,' she says, in a hoarse kind of voice. 'I didn't want him to die. Not really. Not like this. I didn't mean . . . I never thought it would be like this. I only wanted him to—' She breaks off, and turns round, looking for Shaw. 'Do you understand?' she asks him. 'Do you understand I didn't mean it?'

But he only shrugs, and lights another cigarette.

My sister turns her wild eyes, then, on the rat catcher. 'Surely,' she says. 'Surely you understand?'

I thought, previously, that his features had been so ravaged as to render him incapable of any kind of expression. And yet, while I could be imagining it, what with the flickering firelight and the awful smoke wafting in tendrils all around us, there is surely some kind of pain there in his face as he returns her gaze.

'I couldn't say,' he says. 'I understand all sorts of things – what makes the lowliest, most disgusting beasts upon this earth do the things they do – but even understanding them, I still set the traps, and I still put down the poison.'

Then he turns away from her, to look out over the parks.

She speaks to me after that. 'Brother,' she says, 'please believe me. I'm sorry.'

I find I don't know what to tell her. I simply stare, uncertain, back, until I cannot meet her eyes a moment longer and return to watching the fire and the crone, who is still consumed with laying her stones, one by one around the edge.

My sister starts to cry. Softly at first, but then more extremely, until she seems quite taken over by the force of it.

She is left alone to howl like that until the old woman lays the last stone of her circle. Then she straightens up, the crone, and with the same terrible slowness that characterises all her movements she hobbles her way across the flagstones to lay a hand upon my sister's shoulder. There's a moment when I think Ethel might be about to throw her off, and dismiss her as she tried to dismiss Shaw, but then, still sobbing, she clutches at her mother's hand and sinks into her arms.

I watch them there together for a while until suddenly I find I am incontrovertibly tired of them, and tired of everyone, at the same time as feeling strangely light within myself as a vessel newly emptied, ready to be filled up to the brim again. I get to my feet and shake the worst of the ash from my clothes.

The rat catcher – the burning man, that murderous and vengeful spectre that so haunted my imaginings – has his back to me now, still staring out over the battlements.

'Rat Catcher,' I say. 'Thank you, for helping me like that. For helping my father. Goodness knows I did not deserve so much.'

He turns, and the sight of his face there with all its crags and peeling, melted skin lit up by the morning sun doesn't fill me with horror, or fear; it doesn't even make me shiver.

'I only did what needed to be done, Your Majesty,' he says.

I find myself smiling at that. 'Long may you continue to do so, Mr Rat Catcher,' is all that I can manage to say.

He tips me a nod, and I find myself wondering if we are almost comrades now – or at least if there is some thread of understanding that connects us, however fragile it may be. His coat billows out behind him in the breeze then, and I see that he reminds me of those dark birds that so frightened me before, as I hid out in the forest.

I whisper a last farewell into flames – which are dying now, the process almost at its end – and I finally turn from the brightness of the battlements, and slowly make my way back down the stairs. It's not until I'm in the entrance hall, standing alone at the foot of its vast, marble stairs, that it occurs to me it might be time I did something about the palace, and began to take some care of it again. I shall open all the windows, I resolve, and then find the rat catcher some help in his work, so that he may truly rid it of its vermin.

Before I begin upon any of that, though, I realise that there is one more thing I have to see to in the woods, for I am conscious, now, of having kept my little Luke waiting for me far too long. I shall wash my hands, I decide, and wash my face, and put on a proper suit of clothes, and then I shall walk out into the trees one last time, all the way back to my cabin, where I shall give Luke the proper burial that such a gentle, harmless creature as he was deserves.

Acknowledgements

Thank you so much to my agent, Peter Straus, and to my editor, Mary-Anne Harrington. Thank you to Yeti, for the beautiful cover, to Amy Perkins, and to everyone at Tinder Press. Thank you to Matthew Turner, Eliza Plowden, Laurence Laluyaux, Stephen Edwards and everyone at Rogers, Coleridge & White. Thank you to Andrew Cowan, Philip Langeskov, Naomi Wood, Grace Brown, Sarah Hopkinson, Cara Marks, Benjamin S. Morrison, Victoria Proctor, Fiona Sinclair and all my incredible UEA tutors and friends. Thank you to Niamh and the whole MacSweeney family for all the support and inspiring microadventures. Thank you to Ivana Prekopova for the sanity, kindness and wisdom. Thank you to Jakob Tanner and Jessica Johannesson Gaitán for reading early drafts. Thank you to my brilliant friends and former colleagues at Mr B's Emporium, to all the UCL Writers' Society people from back in the day, and to all my wonderful friends in Bath, London and Norwich. Thank you so much and all my love to Ben Noble – and to my parents, Lorna and Kazuo Ishiguro.

A Q&A with Naomi Ishiguro

Some of the stories, like 'Wizards' and 'Shearing Season', are seen through the eyes of a child. Do you feel children have a different, more magical perspective on the world?

Obviously kids have a completely different perspective on the world. I'm not sure if it's necessarily more magical though . . . I just think childhood is such an interesting time to write about, in that it's when a person's sense of self is most likely to be in flux, and at its most fragile in some ways, at its most resilient in others, and generally at its most open to the possibility of change.

Really, if the *Escape Routes* stories do anything, I'd like them to remind readers of how it felt to have that sense of openness, and also remind people of that resilience in the face of change that so often comes with childhood. I'd love if the stories could take people back to a time in which they were used to being surprised and transformed by the process of encountering new things in the world.

Throughout the collection, there is a sense of cities being a trap and the countryside offering freedom, particularly in 'Heart Problems' and 'Accelerate!'. Why do you think this is such a powerful image and message?

I can only hope it's a powerful message. It's certainly something very close to my heart, as someone who grew up in London, and who was only passingly aware of things like the cycle of the seasons, or of how many different animal, insect, bird and plant species there are out there still in spite of the ecological crisis. Leaving London in my twenties and having a bit of a crash course in the natural world honestly felt like freeing myself from a particularly poisonous world-view. It was as if a new part of my mind had been unlocked, and my whole perspective on the world – and on the way humans exist within it – altered to become something which I hope is much realer, healthier, and better-informed. I do absolutely think that that's a very real kind of freedom that the countryside can offer – the freedom to see things more clearly, maybe. Hopefully this perspective-shift is something readers will be able to relate to. I do also think it's just generally so important for us all to keep questioning the priorities and values that are so enshrined in all these extreme urban models of living, and to ask whether those ways of life can actually bring us any real freedom or happiness at all.

Although the natural world offers freedom, it is also volatile and unknown. Could you elaborate on the double standard of freedom in the collection?

There's a version of the idea of freedom which involves being untethered, and without obligations, commitments or familiarity. More often than not, this kind of 'freedom' also necessarily involves being without a support network, and without any of those ties which keep many of us grounded in society and generally looked-after. While writing these stories I was thinking a lot about Jon Krakauer's *Into the Wild*, and the hugely sad story it tells of what happened to Christopher McCandless. It seemed to me like such a horrible irony – that someone could sever all ties and literally walk out of his comfort zones in an effort to find a kind of 'pure' freedom, only to end up in a new unforeseen trap.

In a lot of my stories, the characters' efforts to free them-selves from all earthly ties end in a kind of dissolving of self – in a sublimation of their individual lives and personal iden-tities into the natural world. That's kind of how I interpret the *Into the Wild* narrative, too, in that the logical conclusion of that kind of search for freedom seems to be a kind of collapsing of one's sense of self into something impersonal: something much bigger than any human individual, that can transcend all ties, traumas and emotional obligations. That kind of dissolution of self is, of course, just a hair's breadth away from death – which could be a type of freedom in itself, but only the most tragic kind. So yes, there's definitely a double-standard to the way I write about freedom in the collection in that regard.

The symbol of birds appears in many of the stories. What attracted you to this image in particular?

Obviously birds are generally very useful universal symbols for freedom and flight. More specifically though, the prepon-derance of birds in this collection is probably down to the fact that 'The Flat Roof' was the first of these stories I wrote, and I literally wrote it surrounded by birds, sitting on the flat roof of the block of flats where I lived. I was particularly drawn to the idea that while the birds and I were momentarily sharing the same physical space, the birds would obviously have such a different view of the city from my human perspective. I love the idea that while birds can travel huge distances and see the world on a similar scale to humans, they move through the world without any human sense of ownership or trespass, or of borders, states, or immigration rules.

I also love Old English poetry – the really old stuff from before the Norman Conquest – and birds often show up in those poems as images of a soul freed from the earthly shackles of material existence – something which obviously relates to that *Into the Wild* idea of freedom again, and that ascetic negating of self. I often use birds as an externalisation of a character's yearning for that kind of release. I like how framing that yearning in the context of earthly yet distant things, like birds, can make it seem all at once almost tangible, and yet still impossibly unattainable.

I also love the image of a murmuration of starlings as an analogue for a short story collection, in that a murmuration involves a number of individual, separate parts working together to form an almost ghostly image of a wider, greater whole.

Most of the stories are firmly rooted in the real world with just a hint of magic. This combination offers characters a

moment of transformation. What do you think this type of fiction can offer readers in today's often confusing world?

Probably not a massive amount! I mean, we certainly need a lot more than a set of short stories to help navigate the world right now. But if anyone reads the stories and is reminded of a time in their lives when they believed change was possible, and believed in the possibility of transformative miracles both personal and political, then I'll be delighted. For me, magic in books works best when it puts us back in touch with a sense of wonder. Wonder in general is so under-rated. It sounds impossibly cheesy but I really do believe it expands our capacity for empathy, and helps us dream of better worlds.

The collection is woven together by three linked fairy tales about a rotten kingdom. What about this story did you feel tied all the others together?

I liked the idea of weaving all the stories together into a fairy tale framework, as hopefully the effect is to cast all the other more real-world stories as fairy tales or fables too. I also liked the idea of those three more overt fairy tales acting as a kind of Gothic mirror to the other more 'normal' stories, with the images of birds in the 'normal' stories reincarnating as rats in the mad Gothic ones.

Those three fairytales also have the overall narrative shape of a 'coming of age'/'assuming responsibility for a bewildering and broken world', and I wanted that thread running through the whole book, as all the stories are really in some way about young people figuring these things out in various ways.

I hear you're working on a novel. Can you tell us anything about it?

Yes! It's coming out with Tinder Press in the late spring of 2021, and I'm very excited about it indeed. I don't want to say too much, but it's much more social realist than *Escape Routes*, and it's basically about two friends from very different worlds who meet by chance on a common as young teenagers. The novel then follows them into adulthood, and looks at the difficulty of maintaining friendships across the vast social divides that exist in Britain today.

Cunning Folk is an independent magazine with a focus on folklore, the occult, and magic in our world today.
Get a copy from cunning-folk.com

Molly Aitken is the author of *The Island Child*.